FAMILY SECRETS

SHORT STORIES

Betsey Barber Hampton

FAMILY SECRETS: Short Stories

Cover art: Brad Stiller

Merlin-Janus Studio

Mooresville, NC

Publishing History

First Edition 2017

Print ISBN: 978-0692958025

Published in the United States of America

FAMILY SECRETS

Family Secrets	5
Coming About	18
Murder on South Street	28
A Family Affair	35
Special Delivery	49
Daddy's Girl	57
Jenny's Secret Love	72
Gene Pool	79
Lost	90
Jon and Jessica	100
Chartreuse Bike	111
Living in Technicolor	119
Double Trouble	132
Midlife Crisis	149

FAMILY SECRETS

The road wound around a lake and up a hill to a deserted old house almost hidden beneath giant oak trees. As soon as I pulled in front, I felt a connection—like this house was waiting for something to happen, like we had been waiting for each other.

It was no ordinary house. I loved its charm and beauty and wondered who built it. I sensed that love went in with every nail, and I wondered if the owner had been happy here, raised children here, and why it was so neglected. Walker-Kline Realty was the name on the sign in the front yard.

"My name is Sunny Myers," I told the receptionist when I called. "I'm interested in one of your listings." She transferred my call to Charlie Kline, who told me the present owners inherited the house, that they hated it and never intended to live in it.

"They'll accept just about any price to get rid of it," he said, "but it needs a lot of work. When do you and your husband want to see it?"

"I don't have a husband, Mr. Kline, but I would like to see it at your earliest convenience."

I detected a tone of dismissal in his voice when he said, "This is not an area where a woman should live alone. Besides, the house needs someone with a lot of money to restore it."

"I still want to see the house, Mr. Kline," I replied angrily.

The yard proved to be as neglected as the house. A once beautiful brick walk was hidden beneath the overgrown weeds that escaped between its crevices and around its borders. The pink roses climbing a trellis at the front door had not been pruned in years.

When Charlie opened the door, we were met by the smell of old wood and the faint aroma of ashes from the fireplaces.

A center hall ran the length of the house. To the left of the foyer was a parlor with wide plank flooring marred by years of scratches and heel marks. The plastered walls were streaked with cracks. A brick fireplace with an arched opening had a hand-carved mantle with delicate scroll work that had been painted white.

Beyond the parlor was a banquet-sized dining room, and in the center, a crystal chandelier hung from an ornate ceiling medallion. Heavy paneled doors led to an outdated kitchen.

The fireplace in the library would need to be rebuilt, while the rich cherry wood paneling and floor-to-ceiling book cases required refinishing. Last but not least, a sunroom, bedroom, and bath completed the lower level.

A beautiful newel post topped with a large round finial stood before the stairs leading to four bedrooms on the second floor.

A flower garden, now deserted but for an angel statue and a gray weathered bench, was located just behind the house. The yard then sloped gently down to a lake, where a boathouse, almost a miniature of the big house, stood at a pier extending over the water.

The romance of the place appealed to me because I am a writer, best known for a mystery series. The novels feature Jonas Frye, a photographer who records murder scenes for the police. Jonas and his detective friend, Sinclair, solve the mysteries and bring the killers to justice.

The income from my books would allow me to buy the house and restore it to its original beauty. I liked the fact that it was secluded and I could work in peace, with no nosey neighbors popping in and out, but something else was drawing me there.

Charlie Kline assured me that it was structurally sound and everything in working order. I made an offer, and after one counter offer, to which I agreed, the place was mine. Then I *really* wanted to know its history.

Charlie gave me the number of a good contractor named Danny Fuller, an African American. "He lives right across the lake from you," Charlie added. "Danny is the best around, so you would be lucky to get him."

Danny proved to be tall, slender, and light-skinned with a dimple in his chin. He wore khaki pants and a green shirt that brought out the green flecks in his golden brown eyes. I thought he belonged on the cover of a magazine as I reached out to take his card: Daniel J. Fuller, Construction and Restorations.

"I always loved this old house," he said. "It belonged to John Carl Scott, we called him J.C. You might have heard of him. He was a star basketball player in his college days. Later, he owned Scott Construction and he built this house for his wife, Franny. It was his pride and joy. He called it *Rose Point.*

"His son Bo and I were best friends," Danny continued. We played together, fished together, and pretty much did everything together, so I spent a lot of my childhood here. I'd love the chance to bring it back to life, but it will be a long and tedious job. If you agree to my estimate, I promise you'll be sick of me and my mess before I'm done."

Danny went from room to room making notes of what needed to be done and a list of supplies he had to buy. We ended up in the attic, where he wanted to check for leaks in the roof. The heat sucked the breath from my lungs and refilled them with ancient dust.

"My God!" Danny exclaimed, brushing away spider webs. "I can't believe that Scott's stuff is still up here." He picked up a deflated basketball. "Look, it's the basketball we used to play with." Then, he picked up a portrait and wiped away the dust.

"Who is that man?" I asked.

"That's J.C., Bo's daddy," he said wistfully.

I intended to do my writing in the library, so I asked Danny to begin there. He was almost as anxious as I was to get started. His employees began refinishing the cherry-paneled walls and bookcases, while Danny rebuilt the fireplace. After several weeks of noise and disruption, Danny came out to the sunroom where I was working and said, "I want to get you into the library before cold weather sets in so you can write by a nice warm fire. Do you have time to look at some paint samples?"

He spread the paint chips across the kitchen table. I opened two beers, took a chunk of cheese from the fridge and set out crackers and nuts. "I want to make the restoration as authentic as possible," I said, "so help me pick out the original colors, if you remember."

After pouring over the samples a good long while, Danny finally decided that he could blend two colors to match the original. When he stood up to leave, he said, "Sunny, am I driving you crazy yet?"

I laughed. "Pretty close to it. I am eating, breathing and covered in your dust."

"Tell you what," he said, "let me make it up to you. Tomorrow I'll show you around the lake and then cook chicken on the grill. I'll pick you up in my boat at 6:00 and get you out of here for a while. Dress casual," he advised.

The next evening, after I had bathed and washed my hair, I felt almost human again. The sun was setting and cool air blew across my face as Danny steered the boat across the lake, tied up to his pier, and led me to a picnic table under some shade trees.

A fuzzy little mutt named Handsome came running out to meet us. I drank the wine Danny had poured me, while he cooked chicken and baked potatoes. He talked about the house—how great it was looking and how happy J. C. would be to witness its rebirth.

It was dark when he took me home, using a lantern in the boat's bow to light the way. After tying up to the dock, he took my hand and helped me up onto the pier.

"Somebody's been hanging around here." He frowned. "Sunny, I've noticed some cigarette butts, and things have been moved out of place in the boathouse. I hope it's safe for you to live here alone," he said as he walked me to the house.

"Don't worry, I can take care of myself," I answered flippantly.

But the very next morning when I stepped out the back door I stumbled on a broken brick. My ankle gave way and I fell to the ground, crying out in pain. The only thing I could do was crawl to the steps and wait for Danny to come to work.

When he arrived, his face creased with worry, he examined my foot and explained, "It's not your ankle, it's your arch. It needs to be x-rayed, so we're going to the doctor now," he insisted as he helped me to his truck.

I came home with a cast, crutches and pain meds. Danny put me in the sunroom with my foot propped up, gave me a pill, and started working in the library. I was so out of it, I barely heard the construction noise. Danny brought my food in for a couple of days, using his key to let himself in and out. I kept waiting for another lecture about not being safe here, but I think he knew me well enough by then to know his words would be wasted.

Finally, I was able to walk into the restored library to watch the men place my oriental rug on newly refinished floors that smelled like wood polish and wax. They moved in the furniture, my TV, and hooked up my computer. Danny carried in my mahogany grandfather clock, set it to the proper time, and then brought in an armload of wood to build a fire.

"I plan to eat a bowl of chili here in front of the fire," I said." Please stay and have some with me, Danny."

I was admiring my new work space as we ate, when suddenly Danny asked, "What is your next book going to be about?"

"So far nothing I write is working," I admitted. "I've started over three times. I need a new idea—a murder, a body—anything to get me started."

Several days later, Danny's men began working in the parlor. They had stripped the white paint off the mantle, revealing a rich golden wood. The next step was to apply a clear coat of lacquer, so Danny went down to the boat house, where he kept his supplies.

Suddenly, I heard him rush back in, calling my name.

"What's" wrong?" I asked.

"It's in the boathouse!" he shouted in obvious panic.

"What are you talking about?"

"That body you wanted for inspiration! Hurry, call the police!"

"What did it look like?"

"*It* looked like a *dead girl*!"

I picked up the phone and dialed 911.

Soon the police were swarming all around the boathouse, taking photos, fingerprints, and looking for clues. We watched as the corpse was brought up on a gurney and loaded into an ambulance. "Poor girl," Danny moaned. "Who would want to kill her, and what the hell was she was doing in your boathouse?"

Later, the police came to the door and scowled at Danny. "She died from a blow to the head with a blunt instrument," they told us both. "We suspect she had been raped, but we'll have to do more tests. Mr. Fuller, we will definitely want to talk to you again, so we'll be back in touch."

"Just wait," Danny said after they left. "Those police are going to blame me."

"Calm down. Why do you think that?"

"Because, they always think African American men are rapist."

I thought he was being paranoid, but what did I know? The only true crime experience I had was the fiction between the covers of my books.

Sure enough, the very next day Danny had just spread the panel doors over saw horses and was sanding them when the police showed up asking for him: "Sorry, Mr. Fuller, but we have to take you down to the station. Turns out the girl was killed with a hammer found in the boathouse, and it had your fingerprints all over it. She was pregnant. Is that why you killed her?"

Danny almost collapsed from shock and fear. His hand trembled as he removed his tool belt and handed it to me, along with the keys to his house. "Will you take care of Handsome?" he begged.

"I'll hire a lawyer, try not to worry," I said, hoping to reassure him. "I'll see you in the morning. Promise."

That afternoon when I got to Danny's house I found a leash, a bag of dog food, and headed to my car with Handsome. A woman next door waved, so I walked over to tell her what was going on.

"I tell you, ma'am, Danny didn't kill nobody," she said angrily. That dead girl lived about a mile on down this road. You need to go talk to her mama."

I made Handsome a bed near my fire and looked up the number of a good attorney I knew, then called the jail. I learned that Danny would be arraigned the next day at 1:00. At that time, his bail would be set.

Next I went to see the dead girl's mother.

"My daughter was dating a white boy," the woman told me. "The boy's father was furious, said he was going to put a stop it one way or another. I been telling her she was playing with fire. Sure enough she got pregnant. She said they were going to run away together."

The woman handed me a note she had found among her daughter's things: *Meet me at the boat house tonight at 8:00, and let's talk about what we're gonna do. Love, Billy.*

I convinced the woman to accompany me to the attorney's office with the note. Once the lawyer had examined it, the three of us went to see the judge, who then ordered that Danny be released.

When the jailor unlocked his cell, I put my arms around Danny and said, "You can go home now."

In the car, I told him about my visit to see the girl's mother and the note she had found. His hands shook as he stared straight ahead and said, "thank you, Sunny."

As soon as we walked in the house, Handsome jumped all over him. "I'm glad to see you, too, buddy. I missed you!" he said. I knew Danny needed a drink, so I told him to wait in the library while I got some wine.

The night before, out of curiosity, I had returned to the attic and discovered a box of old photos. One was of Danny on the pier, fishing with Bo. Danny must have been about six. He had lost his two front teeth, and he was proudly holding up a little fish in front of the camera.

I had then taken that photo and J.C.'s portrait to the library, hung the portrait over the mantel and casually left the photo on the coffee table.

Now, as I handed Danny a glass of wine and sat on the sofa beside him, he already had the photograph in hand and was close to tears. I put my arm around him. "Danny, what's wrong?" I asked.

"I need to get something off my chest," he admitted, then cleared his throat. "You are the only person in the world I've ever told, Sunny, but J.C. was my daddy."

I gasped. When I finally found the words, I whispered, "How do you know?"

"Mama told me the truth soon after J.C. died. The man I thought was my daddy left right after I was born. Then while I was growing up, J.C. treated me pretty much like he treated Bo. I just assumed J.C. felt sorry for me. He gave me the canoe he'd had when he was a boy so I could row across the lake and play with Bo. I was always welcome...

"This place was like my second home. When Bo and I got into fights, J.C. disciplined us equally. He taught me how to fish, swim, play basketball, and how to work and save my money. Without J.C.'s influence, I might have been breaking into houses and stealing cars. He taught me right from wrong."

Danny paused to get his emotions under control, while I struggled to absorb this amazing news and pour us more wine. "Were you and Bo much alike?" I asked.

"Not really, Sunny," Danny answered. "Bo was not athletic like me. He was short like his mother, but his spirit was ten feet tall. All he ever wanted was to be a pilot, so right after high school he joined the Air Force. Then tragically, several years after he joined, he crashed in the desert. His body was never recovered, and his poor mother, Franny, grieved herself to death.

"I also graduated soon after Bo joined the Air Force. J.C. put me to work on one of his construction crews, where I figured I'd stay the rest of my life. But after he lost Bo and Franny, he turned his attention to me.

"One day he called me to his office to tell me he was sending me to college. He didn't ask if I wanted to go, he simply said, 'I got you a basketball scholarship.' Soon after that he sent me off in a beat up old red truck, with Scott Construction painted on its side."

"What a wonderful story, Danny! How did college go?"

"Well, I played basketball all four years, and I was pretty good. I guess I inherited J.C.'s skills and his love for the game, but I'm sure my African American Achilles tendons and my wide wing span helped some, too." He paused and grinned bashfully. "Not to brag, but I could jump higher than any white boy on the team. J.C. would attend a game and afterwards critique me: 'you need to get more rebounds, son. After all, you're the tallest boy on the team. Work at improving your speed in transition and stop being so shy, try more three pointers'."

"And all that time you never once suspected?" I wondered.

"No, I never dreamed that J.C. was anything more than my mentor and friend. He continued to encourage me when I decided to be an architect, but later changed my mind. Finally I took a class in historic restoration, which peaked my interest, then after graduation, J. C. put me back to work at Scott Construction. Although I learned the business end of things, I was best at restorations. Once I heard J.C. tell a customer, 'Let my Danny take a look at that. I'll send him to you right away.' Then J.C. would check my progress every few days, and when I finished, he would say, 'Damn good job, Danny!'"

"He was so proud of you! That had to feel good."

Danny smiled and nodded. "I drove that little old red truck until the wheels fell off, and then J.C. gave me a brand new one."

"What did your mother tell you about *her* relationship with J. C.?"

"She told me that J.C.'s wife Franny suffered from epilepsy. Sometimes after a seizure, she would be in bed for days. It got worse as she aged. J. C. was terribly lonely, so he and Mama started meeting in the boathouse. At first she thought they were just two young people

16

having a fling, but it turned into much more and lasted for years. I was their 'little secret,' she said.

"J. C. didn't have any family except a sister, Colleen, whom he didn't like very much. After he had a stroke, Colleen put him into a nursing home, then she and his attorney sold his business and his house.

"Sometimes after work, I would visit and feed him supper. He was trapped inside his body, unable to talk, but his doctor assured me he could hear. And when I thanked him for all he'd done for me, he would look into my eyes and squeeze my hand."

Danny stretched out his long legs, crossed them at the ankles, and continued, "J. C. put his whole life into this place, and it made me sick to stand by and watch people destroy it. I wanted to buy it and save it, to make him proud of me, but I couldn't afford to. Then destiny stepped in and brought you here. I wish J. C. could see what you've done, Sunny."

"What *you've* done Danny!" I glanced up at the portrait and said, "Damn good job, right J. C.?"

That's when I noticed the little dimple in J.C.'s chin. I blew a kiss to the portrait and said, "Sir, I know all about your lovemaking in the boathouse and your 'little secret.' In fact, he's sitting right here beside me, and you'll be happy to know that he turned out real good—a lot like his daddy."

The room was quiet for a few minutes. All we heard was the ticking of the grandfather clock and Handsome licking himself.

Then Danny wiped a tear from my cheek. I felt his warm breath on my neck as he drew me close and bent his head to kiss me. And in case you wonder what happened next—well, that's our "little secret."

COMING ABOUT

Just after sunup on a hot August morning, I was listening to birds chirping in the old oak tree outside my bedroom window when I heard a crash coming from the kitchen. Uncle Al was making his breakfast, which hadn't changed in all his sixty-eight years: strong black coffee, three strips of bacon and two fried eggs placed between two slices of white bread toasted to a golden brown. One strip of bacon was for Mo, his golden retriever.

The food on his plate was still warm. He was lying on the floor with Mo licking his face. The dog already knew what I would find out when the medics arrived.

My uncle was good to me, but very strict: children should be seen, not heard and never ask questions. When we did ask questions, Uncle Al would say, "That's for me to know and you to find out."

My parents, Mary and Clifford Hall, died in an automobile accident when I was only one year old. Uncle Al, Daddy's brother, raised me with help from his old maid sister, Rosa. When I was old enough to go to school,

Rosa answered the Lord's call to become a missionary in Africa. Eventually she also died.

With Uncle Al dead, suddenly I was alone with Mo in our old house on Church Street in downtown Charlotte. It was an aging structure surrounded by a rusty wrought iron fence with a squeaky gate that wouldn't close because I used to swing on it. A huge Magnolia tree in the front yard had pushed its roots under the sidewalk, cracking it in two places.

Known to Charlotte Historians as the Hall House, it had an official plaque beside the front door from the Historical Preservation Society. The Hall House was in need of major repairs that I would never be able to afford. Even if I had the money, the Historical Society would be picky about every little detail.

My house had been a Victorian beauty in its day, with a wrap-around porch laced with gingerbread. The turrets on either side of the second story gave it a castle-like appearance. The peaked roof leaked into strategically placed pots in all the upstairs bedrooms, where wallpaper peeled off the walls in great sheets. Outside, the grayish-green paint accented with olive green, burgundy and a soft ivory, needed scraping and a fresh coat.

Uncle Al was buried down the street in the Presbyterian cemetery alongside Mama, Daddy, Aunt Rosa and a forgotten child known only as Baby Girl Hall. I was left wondering what in the devil to do next. When I had time to catch my breath and think, I looked in Uncle Al's wardrobe and found the key to his safe deposit box, which was located in a bank down on Tryon Street.

When I went to the bank, an older woman dressed in purple, with little glasses hanging on a gold chain around her neck, informed me that because I was not listed on Uncle Al's account, I was not allowed to open the box. "His attorney, Mr. Michael Cunningham, is authorized," the woman said, but quickly added, "He's dead."

The Cunningham Law Firm was located only two blocks away, so I walked down Tryon Street. I took the elevator to the sixth floor of the tall office building, then opened a door baring the gold letters: *Cunningham Law Firm*.

I explained my predicament to the secretary and she politely informed me that Mr. Cunningham's son, Christopher, could help. "He will have to meet you at the bank," she said. "Will Wednesday at 1:00 work for you?"

On Wednesday, Christopher Cunningham showed up in a tan suit, white shirt and a burgundy tie, a little wilted from the heat. He brushed his hand through hair streaked with blond by the hot August sun, and I pictured how at home he would look on Lake Norman— in a sailboat.

He shook my hand and then asked the bank employee to let us into the safe deposit vault. We sat at a small table, where the employee placed box #254 between us. Using two keys, his and Uncle Al's, he opened the box.

My uncle's will was right on top. The lawyer read it to me and informed me that I was now the official owner of my dilapidated old house full of dusty antique furniture, a grotesque pea green El Dorado Cadillac that smelled like cigarette smoke, and enough money to cover Uncle Al's burial expenses.

Christopher Cunningham had a habit of saying *hmph*, and I laughed when he said, "Hmph, here are your adoption papers."

"Oh, I'm not *adopted*," I said empathetically as I read the yellowed certificate he handed me:

Certificate of Adoption.

This is to certify that Erin and Ellen Ashton have been formally adopted by Clifford and Mary Hall on this 8th day of June, 1950. Signed by the birth mother, Emma Ashton—the adoptive parents, Clifford Hall and Mary Hall--Witnessed by Dr. Andrew Malone, attending physician of Mercy Hospital—and Michael Cunningham, Attorney at Law.

My breath almost left my body and my heart pounded like a beating drum. I put my head down on the table. In what sounded like a whisper from some faraway place, I heard Christopher Cunningham say, "Miss Hall, are you all right? This must be quite a shock. It *will* take some getting used to. Miss Hall are you all right?"

"Yes," I gasped. "I think I'm okay."

I sat in a state of shock as he leafed through the remaining contents in the box. I don't remember anything until he said, "Hmph, Miss Hall is there someone I can call to walk you home?"

"No. There's no one."

"I'm sure you have a lot of questions. I do have a file on your uncle Albert Hall in my father's file cabinet. It may hold some answers. I'll look through it when I return to the office."

Mo met me at the door with his sad eyes, and I knew he was missing Uncle Al. He sat on the sofa beside me while I explained to him that we were all alone. Uncle Al would not be coming back, and now we owned all this old stuff that I didn't know what the hell to do with. Furthermore, I didn't even know who the hell I was anymore.

Christopher Cunningham's secretary called the next morning. "Mr. Cunningham would like to see you. Can you come in this afternoon at 4PM?"

I put on my yellow and white stripped sundress, walked downtown, took the elevator to the sixth floor and entered the Cunningham Law Firm. Miss Willard explained that the attorney was currently helping a couple with estate planning, but he would be with me shortly. I didn't have to wait long before she ushered me into his office.

Christopher Cunningham sat at a walnut desk in front of a portrait that I assumed was his father. On either side were windows that framed the Charlotte skyline. He stood up and shook my hand. "Miss Hall, may I have Miss Willard bring you something cool to drink?"

He made the *hmph* noise deep in his throat as he opened a folder on the desk. "This is Albert Hall's file. It contains a copy of the adoption papers, but not much else."

"I really had a *twin sister*?" I asked incredulously after reading the contents.

"Yes, you did. I think it would be interesting to see the birth certificates. Shall we walk down to the Register of Deeds office and take a look?"

The deeds clerk handed us a book listing the 1950 births, and under June we found what we were looking for: *June 1, 1950, born to Emma Ashton conjoined twin girls Erin and Ellen Ashton, mother unwed, no father listed.*

My legs got wobbly. I reached out for Christopher's arm to steady myself and he helped me to a chair. I sat and waited while the clerk located the death certificates for Clifford and Mary Hall. She brought a thick book and flipped through until she found Hall. "Yes, here they are. Clifford Hall, Mary Hall, and baby Ellen Hall. They all died January 12, 1952—cause of death was an automobile accident."

Although I'd always known how my "parents" died, I could not stop the tears streaming down my face. Certainly I never knew I had a twin sister who died with them. Christopher Cunningham put his arm around me and whispered, "I'm so sorry. Let's go to the deli in Latta Arcade to have a glass of wine and talk about what to do next."

Several days later, Christopher called. "I have some news. Can you meet me at the oriental restaurant near the office?"

I found him waiting for me at a quiet little table in the corner.

"Erin, I went to Mercy Hospital and did some research. When I looked through the archives, I found the name and address of now-retired Dr. Andrew Malone. I called, and he remembers delivering you and Ellen.

"Dr. Malone told me he had delivered hundreds of babies, but only one set of conjoined twins. He said, '*Who could forget them? They were joined at the hip.*' He had to perform a Caesarian section. You two were premature and lived in an incubator until you were out of danger. The doctor described you as '*poor little things who would never be able to live a normal life.*'

"Your mother was an unwed twenty- year-old who had no way to care for her girls, so she readily agreed to have them adopted. But no one wanted conjoined twins.

"The doctor explained that one of the nurses, Mary Hall, cared for you until you were old enough to go home, but you had no home to go to. Nurse Mary had become so attached to you both, that she and her husband Clifford decided to adopt. My father, Michael Cunningham, represented the Hall family.

"Dr. Malone believed it would be a simple procedure to separate the two of you, but no one was willing to take the chance except the Halls. And back in those days, few people could afford to pay for that surgery. So your adoptive parents waited until you were a year old, then took you to Philadelphia for the operation.

"The Philadelphia doctors kept you until you were healing well, then you were released on a cold January day. On your way home, your car skidded on an icy road. You were the only one who survived, Erin. The tragic accident was covered by The Charlotte Observer.

"*Such a sad story,*' Dr. Malone said. '*After all they had been through, to have that happen, it just broke my heart. Mary Hall was a wonderful woman and a great nurse. I remember attending the funeral.*"

Christopher paused in his long recitation to gaze into my eyes. "Dr. Malone really wants to meet you, Erin. I told him we would come Friday after work. Is that okay with you? Afterwards, we could go to my cabin on Lake Norman, for a swim and a sail in my boat."

I was so moved, and frankly stunned, by everything I had just heard that I hardly knew how to respond. Finally I managed to say, "I'd love to meet Dr. Malone, but I don't own a swim suit." I did not tell him I had never worn one because I was embarrassed about the scar on my hip.

"Well, I think it's high time you got a swim suit," Christopher said. "I could go down to Ivey's with you and help you choose one. Do you want me to do that?"

"No thanks, Christopher." I smiled at the silly idea. "I can manage that much on my own, and I'll be ready on Friday."

On Friday, Dr. Malone's male attendant answered the door. "The doctor is anxiously awaiting your arrival," he said as he led us into a room, where we found Dr. Malone in a wheelchair.

"Hello, Doctor," Christopher said. "This is Miss Erin Hall. I believe you two have met before."

Doctor Malone grabbed my hand and kissed it. "Yes, indeed, my dear, I am delighted to see you again. It has been a very long time, and I have wondered about you through the years. I am so sorry you lost your parents and sister in that horrible wreck. I suppose you were not injured?"

"My Uncle told me the scar on my hip was from an injury I sustained in the wreck, but now I know the truth. It was from the separation surgery. But tell me, Doctor, do you remember my mother?"

"Oh yes, my dear. Your mother, Emma Ashton, was a cheeky young thing, but I know nothing about her family because no family member ever showed up. I do know Emma was determined to become an actress, and spunky she was, I imagine she achieved her goal...

"Anyway, an older man accompanied Emma when she came to sign the adoption papers. In her very dramatic way, Emma thanked Mary Hall, wished her good luck, threw back her bleached blond hair, put on her dark glasses and said she was leaving town.

"I don't know if you're planning to look for her," Dr. Malone added, "but I discourage that notion. You are a lovely young woman who has survived against great odds. It's probably best to leave well enough alone and get on with your life, my dear."

With Dr. Malone's words ringing in my ears, I decided to put my thoughts about finding my birth mother on the back burner and take his advice—at least for that day. After all, I had purchased a rose colored swim suit that fit like a glove, with only a small part of my scar showing.

Plus Christopher had insisted on taking Mo with us to the lake, which pleased me. When they met, Mo must have thought Christopher was a reincarnation of Uncle Al, because they became instant friends.

Christopher had promised that Mo would love being free on the lake. Well, that was true enough—for both of us, really. Mo sat up in the bow of the sailboat. His ears blew in the soft breeze as the day faded away, leaving pink and orange streaks across the lake.

In the meantime, I was still trying to process all the things I had learned in the past few weeks and remembered what Dr. Malone had said only a few hours ago: *It's probably best to leave well enough alone and get on with your life, my dear.*

The boat rocked and water splashed against the sides as it encountered another boat's wake. Christopher *came about*, which he explained meant *changing direction*. He adjusted the sails, left the wake behind and set us on a smoother course. Then he turned and smiled at me. "Hmph," he said. "What are you thinking about, Erin Hall?"

.   I looked at the scar peeking from beneath the left leg of my swim suit and smiled back at him. "Life, I guess. I want to come about."

He gave me a thumbs up, then turned back around to be sure we were headed in the right direction.

MURDER ON SOUTH STREET

Jett and Alice were married at 6PM on a chilly October evening in the Presbyterian Church in Carthage, South Carolina.   Alice's ivory satin gown shimmered in the candlelight emanating from candelabra arranged among baskets of sweet smelling flowers at the pulpit. The gown with long sleeves and a high neckline enhanced the pearl necklace her mother and Alice's two had worn as a brides.

Alice's sisters preceded her down the aisle in powder blue dresses with lace inserts and lace sleeves that reached their fingertips. The bride and her sisters carried white calla lilies tied with blue satin ribbons.

Her Aunt Sally played the wedding march as Mr. Cummings escorted his daughter down the aisle to where Jett stood beaming as his lovely bride approached. Soon they would begin their new life together.

After the reception held in the church fellowship hall, Alice changed into her raspberry colored suit with matching hat, placed a fox tail fur around her neck and drove with her husband to their new home in Dickson, a little college town in North Carolina.

Their house, located on South Street next door to the elementary school, was painted mustard yellow trimmed in cinnamon brown and creamy white.

Jett lifted Alice in his arms, carried her over the threshold and down the center hall that ran the length of the house. He paused at the staircase located just outside the kitchen, and then took her up to one of the four bedrooms on the second floor.

They were up early the next morning so that Alice could prepare breakfast. Then they went together to the Presbyterian Church on the college campus, because Jett was extremely eager to show off his new bride.

After all, he was an important person in their town— the town pharmacist. He owned *Dickson Cut Rate* on Main Street. Jett's good friend, Dr. Hugh Whisenant, who rented office space above the pharmacy, was also an important man- about- town.

Dr. Whisenant had a habit of winking his left eye. Whether it was a habit or a tick of some sort, nobody knew, but when Jett introduced Hugh Whisenant to his bride, the doctor winked his left eye and kissed her hand, which Alice found very endearing.

Hugh was an avid Bridge player, as was Jett. They had a foursome including some big wheels from the cotton mill. They met on the last Friday night of every month.

Dickson College was established by Presbyterians who believed in providing a higher education for their elite white sons. Having fun in any form was contrary to

Presbyterian principles, so drinking spirits in Dickson was strictly forbidden. But students could easily cross the county line to obtain them, and did so all the time. They had a little shack on the north end of town where they met to unwind, and God knows, after a week in uptight little Dickson, they needed to unwind.

Matilda Whisenant, Dr. Hugh's wife, was the town's most uptight citizen. Playing cards was a sin in her book, and had she known that Hugh occasionally enjoyed a beer while playing Bridge, she would have "flipped her lid." Matilda unfortunately gained a lot of weight while pregnant with two babies that she immediately lost to diphtheria. After the last baby was buried in the Dickson College Cemetery, she moved from Hugh's bed to a guest room across the hall and kept to herself. A box of chocolates was her constant companion.

By contrast, Alice Jenkins had a perfectly gorgeous figure and loved to show it off in her collection of expensive clothes and hats. She never, ever resisted the impulse to buy a hat. She had a trunk full of them, and her fruitwood armoire, that Jett had sent over from France, contained all the latest fashions, two fur coats and a fox tail stole.

Alice liked to make a grand entrance and insisted on sitting near the front of the Dickson Presbyterian church. Once she made the decision about which hat to wear on Sunday morning, she placed it on her saucy blond curls, pulled a little veil over her violet- colored eyes and looked straight ahead as she walked down the aisle—as though it were a fashion runway. Jett followed, ignoring the tittering little whispers coming from the pews as he passed.

Jett was anxious for his Bridge buddies to meet Alice, although everybody in town already knew who she was. Alice wanted very much to be a perfect hostess and to look the part, so she wore her new cornflower blue dress to greet their guests when they arrived for Friday night Bridge. Rosetta, her maid, left cheese straws, ham biscuits and toasted pecans on the kitchen table for Alice to serve.

Austin Holt and Sinclair White from Delburg Mill arrived shortly after 7PM, then Dr. Hugh rushed in a few minutes later.

"Hugh, you remember my wife, Alice?" asked Jett.

"Yes, yes, of course. How are you my dear, Alice?"

"Just splendid, Doctor, and yourself?"

"Fine, fine my dear," he said as his left eye twitched into a wink

The doctor removed his black felt homburg, revealing hair slicked down with shiny oil highlighting the few gray hairs that were beginning to show in his hair and goatee. The scent of musk and sun-warmed pine wafted by as he moved into the parlor.

Alice moved into the little den between the parlor and dining room. Jett brought in the refreshments, a round of beer and then a second round. She listened as the two Delburg men complained about their lazy employees, Jett complained about his long hours and Dr. Whisenant fussed about his high rent, patients not paying him and being called out all hours of the night.

The doctor was the most talkative. He reminded Alice of an old South Carolina saying: "That man could talk the salt out of the sea."

Jett employed a college student as a soda jerk at his pharmacy. The boy served customers lemonades, limeades and a very special Biltmore ice cream. Alice often visited in the afternoons, especially Wednesdays, to enjoy a cone of the rich, creamy butter pecan she favored.

Jett began to notice that Hugh Whisenant, who took Wednesday afternoon off, always managed to come in at just the right moment to wish Alice, "Good afternoon."

On those occasions, Alice would push a stray curl behind her ear, giggle and reply, "Good afternoon yourself, Doctor."

Alice knew Hugh was an accomplished violin player who was featured in the Dickson College Orchestra. So Alice would giggle again and say, "I am so looking forward to having you play your violin for me. Promise me you will."

Early in April, the Bradford Pear trees all along Main Street burst into bloom, causing Alice's hay fever to act up. Her eyes became red and weepy, her nose ran and she sneezed constantly.

"You should let Hugh have a look at you," Jett urged.

"Yes, of course," she answered.

Hugh prescribed an allergy powder, and Jett filled the order. On the prescription Hugh instructed: "take twice a day, then come back to see me in ten days."

But after ten days the Bradford Pears had dropped their fragrant white blossoms and replaced them with little green leaves. Alice's nose had stopped running and she stopped coming into the pharmacy for her butter pecan ice cream cone on Wednesday afternoons.

From his post at the prescription counter in the back of the pharmacy, Jett looked out the front window to watch the comings and goings of the town's people on Main Street. Every Wednesday afternoon Hugh Whisenant still came down the stairs from his office, stuck his head in the pharmacy door, winked his left eye and wished Jett a good afternoon. Then the doctor would head down Main Street, cross over to South Street and disappear.

This seemed strange, because Dr. Whisenant lived in the opposite direction. His house was located beyond the college and across the street from the Presbyterian Church. It was a big white house with a Mimosa tree leaning against the picket fence bordering Main Street.

One Wednesday afternoon in early June, Hugh came downstairs, opened the squeaky brown door of *Dickson Cute Rate Pharmacy*, winked his left eye and again wished Jett a good afternoon.

"You too, Hugh. Good afternoon, my friend."

Jett watched Hugh cross the street and head toward South Street, but this time, after waiting a few minutes,

Jett took off his white jacket, laid it across his stool and slipped quietly out the back door.

Jett walked up South Street to his own house, and without making any noise at all, he opened the front door and listened. He heard voices coming from upstairs. Alice giggled, and then a man's voice snickered in response.

Jett tip-toed across the parlor carpet, past the green velvet sofa to his desk in the corner, where he very quietly opened the center drawer and removed a pistol.

Just after dark that evening, Hugh Whisenant's body was found in an upstairs bedroom of the Jenkins's house. He was lying across the bed, a bullet in his back just below his right shoulder blade

Dr. Hugh Whisenant was buried in the Dickson College Cemetery beside his two infant daughters.

The county sheriff searched high and low for Jett and Alice Jenkins; to no avail. The couple was never seen or heard from again. But today, a century later, if you visit the Jenkin's house on South Street you will hear soft violin music coming from the upstairs bedroom. And if you are very quiet, you will hear a voice calling, "Alice, where are you Alice?"

A FAMILY AFFAIR

In a desperate letter, my older sister Rosemary wrote: *Cathryn, I miss you. I'm sorry I haven't been in touch. Things are not good here and I am afraid for my future. If you can arrange it, please come for a visit.*

***

Rosemary's life had become a mystery after she eloped with a stranger named John Ratcliff and cut off all communications with her family here in Lake James, North Carolina.

Soon after my sister eloped, her former boyfriend, Lawrence Kincaid, started asking me out. "Lawrence is a fine local boy," my parents said approvingly. "He would be an ideal husband."

But soon after my wedding to Lawrence, I realized I was in a loveless marriage. No matter how hard I tried, I couldn't please my husband.

After four unhappy years, Lawrence suffered a brain aneurysm and was on life support for several weeks. As a dutiful wife, I was determined to take him home and care for him until his doctors finally convinced me that he would remain in a vegetative state for the rest of his life. Finally, I agreed to let them wean him off the tubes and in three days he was dead.

Lawrence's untimely death was a shock. I was exhausted from the funeral and so were my financial resources. With no insurance to cover the mountain of bills, my only option was to put our house on the market and look for a job.

But first, with my sister Rosemary's recent letter nagging, I needed to find out why she sounded so afraid for her future.

After some research, I located Ratcliff Antiques, her husband's business, on a side street in the old section of a little town called Lansdowne. Its stucco façade had a wrought iron balcony wrapped around a second story with three cathedral shaped windows. The front door was set back beneath the balcony under a green sign with white neon lights.

I stood momentarily at the shop window admiring a Queen Ann dining table set with fine English china. Displayed on the sideboard were a silver service, a crystal wine decanter and eight etched wine glasses rimmed with gold. The hands of a grandfather clock in the background pointed to 2pm.

A little bell jingled when I opened the door. Smells of waxed and polished wood filled the air as I entered. Silver tea sets, cut glass pitchers and goblets glistened in the sunlight that came through the front window.

One wall held shelves of dusty books. Some were faded hardbacks, others were bound in soft, worn leather. I imagined the secret notes, treasured photos and long- forgotten bookmarks hidden between their yellowed pages.

Clocks lined another wall. I fancied the timepieces were the centurions that had guarded the lives of generations from birth to death. At the same time, a cold shiver passed through me like an omen warning me of some impending doom straight ahead.

Soon an older woman approached and asked if she could be of help.

"Is Mrs. Rosemary Ratcliff in?" I asked her.

"No, she's not here right now," the woman suspiciously replied.

"Do you expect her soon?"

"No." she answered curtly.

"And Mr. Ratcliff?"

"He will be here soon."

"Then I'll wait," I said nervously.

My brother-in-law entered suddenly through a back door. I was startled by his tortured look—like a dark sinister Heathcliff. He wore riding boots the color of fine aged whisky and a tweet jacket with leather patches on the elbows. He was a tall, slender man with curly black hair brushing the top of his collar. A faint dark stubble covered his chin as he leveled his dark, brooding eyes to meet mine.

I held out my hand, which he refused to take. "John, I am Cathryn Kincaid, Rosemary's sister," I said in spite of the obvious snub. "She asked me to come for a visit, and I told her I would be arriving today."

John Ratcliff had grown up in England. He fixed his black eyes on me and with a gruff, British accent said, "Well, It seems she rather forgot to share that information with me. Were you were planning to stay us?"

"Yes, of course," I replied.

"Well then, I suppose you might as well come back to my office while I call my housekeeper and let her know to expect you."

He led me into a cluttered, dusty room and pulled out a chair. Then he picked up the phone and spoke to someone named Lena. Finally, he turned to me and said in a matter of fact way, "By the way, your sister is missing."

"What do you mean?" I gasped, sinking into the chair.

"She has been gone five days," he sighed. "Naturally, I have asked the police to issue a missing persons alert, but so far there has been no sign of her and no word from her."

When I looked into the black depths of his eyes, I thought, *my sister was afraid of something or someone. Could it be this man, her own husband?*

I followed him home to a stately old brick house that sat in a beautiful wooded area. In the distance, I saw a barn and horses grazing peacefully in a pasture.

When John opened the door, much to my surprise a little girl about three years old ran to him shouting, "Daddy, did you find Mommy today?"

"No, sweetheart, but I will soon. Molly, this is your Aunt Cathryn."

John turned to me and said in a whisper, "We don't go into detail about what has happened around the child. I have tried to keep life as normal as possible, for Molly's sake."

But things aren't normal, I thought as I panicked. *My sister is missing and I didn't even know I had a niece. What the hell have you done to her?*

He poured two glasses of wine from a crystal decanter and handed one to me. "This undoubtedly has proven to be a rather stressful day for you, too. Maybe this will help."

Molly crawled in his lap. He kissed her and brushed back her blond hair. She settled against him and put her thumb in her mouth.

I was nervous as I looked into John's sad eyes and tried make conversation with this complete stranger. I explained that my husband Lawrence had just passed away and that I was selling our house on Lake James.

He seemed shocked. "Lawrence is dead?"

When Lena the housekeeper showed me to the guest room, I asked where my sister had slept. "The master bedroom is Miss Rosemary's," she said. "Mr. Ratcliff sleeps in the one at the end of the hall, next to Molly."

John was gone when I came down to breakfast the next morning, and Lena was feeding Molly. I poured myself a cup of coffee and sat beside them. "Do you know where my mama is?" Molly asked.

My heart was breaking when I answered, "I don't know where she is, Molly, but I'm sure she'll be home soon."

When Molly was out of earshot, I questioned Lena and found out that John raised thoroughbred horses, while the antique shop was mostly Rosemary's business. Apparently she traveled a lot attending estate auctions, yard sales and doing appraisals. This last time when she went on a business trip, she never returned.

I longed to comfort my niece. I spent the day keeping her entertained and her mind off her mother. We were on the back deck—Molly in my lap, sucking her thumb and twisting her hair—when John's car came up the driveway. Molly ran to meet him. He scooped her into his arms and asked, "How's my girl? Did you and Aunt Cathryn have fun today?"

Molly ignored his question, hugged his neck and said, "Did you find Mama?"

I couldn't help but feel compassion for my brother-in-law when I noticed the dark circles under his eyes. He turned his expressionless face to me and said, "Cathryn, there have been some new developments. Come have a drink with me and I'll fill you in."

As I started up the steps, I lost my balance and fell against John. Suddenly, and against my will, I found myself reeling from his nearness. His intoxicating scent and the heat from his body filled my mind with forbidden thoughts. His big hands reached for me. "Careful, Cathryn," he said without emotion.

Once we were settled, he brought me up to date: "We now know Rosemary attended an estate sale in Martinsville, a little mountain town about forty miles north of Lake James. A check she wrote in Martinsville just cleared the bank today.

"Later, after the estate sale, she stopped by the Lake James Tribune and bought several back copies of that paper. The clerk who waited on her recognized her photo from the missing person's report. Now the police are concentrating the search around the Lake James area."

This story was getting crazier by the minute. Rosemary knew I lived in Lake James. Why hadn't she bothered to look me up? Why hadn't she come in person to tell me what she was afraid of? "There is more to this than you are telling me, John. I want to trust you, but I just can't," I told my host.

He gazed at me. "Maybe that will change when you know me better. Can you stay with us a few more days, Cathryn? Until we know what's going on?"

After about a week, Molly was getting less anxious about her mother and was clinging to me more. I had just put her down for an afternoon nap when John came home unexpectedly. He led me to the sofa, a grim look on his face. "Cathryn, I have bad news. I'm afraid Rosemary is dead. Her car was found in Lake James, with her body inside."

I cried uncontrollably. John put his arms around me and stroked my hair. When I finally calmed down, he said, "I must go to the morgue to identify the body. Cathryn, I am so thankful you are here. When I come back, we'll decide together how to tell Molly."

John was visibly shaken when he returned. He poured a glass of straight bourbon and collapsed into his leather chair. "Nobody should ever have to go through this. There will be an autopsy, but it will take two days to get the results." His eyes softened when he looked into mine. "Cathryn, I really don't want to be alone right now, and your niece, poor child, she needs her aunt. Can you stay a little longer?"

Later that afternoon, John closed the antique shop and placed a wreath on the door. We sat down together and planned a funeral at St. Mark's Episcopal Church but we had not yet told Molly.

John picked up his daughter. She twisted her fingers around his curly hair and they headed to the stables. He put her in the saddle, climbed up behind her, and they rode off into the woods.

When they returned, he lifted Molly down into my arms. I could tell by the expressions on both their faces that John had used the outing to tell Molly about her mother's death. I held the child a little tighter as we all walked back towards the stable.

"Mama's in heaven," she told me.

"I'm sure she is, honey," I answered, holding back tears as I set Molly down.

"Mama didn't like horses. Do you like them, Aunt Ryn?"

"Actually, I have never been on a horse," I admitted.

"Daddy can teach you to ride," she offered.

"You bet I can teach you, Aunt *Ryn,*" John said. "Say the word, and we'll have our first lesson."

As he led the mare to her stall, he seemed relieved that the subject of death had been replaced by the fun topic of horses. I decided then and there that I would learn to ride, even if I made a fool of myself.

Later that afternoon John's phone rang. He left the room and was gone a long time. He was pale and his left upper lip twitched when he said, "The autopsy is complete, and they found no indication of foul play. They believe she deliberately drove off the road into the lake. She was pregnant, Cathryn."

For a moment I was too stunned to speak. Finally I said, "My God, John, do you think she deliberately killed herself *and* your baby? What on earth would make her do such a horrible thing?"

He cleared his throat, searching for the right words. "I'm afraid you didn't really know your sister, Ryn. The child was not mine. That much I know. Why she did it, I'm not sure, but I have my suspicions."

"You must tell me everything. Please don't keep secrets from me, John. I want to trust you, I need to trust you."

"I don't want to hurt you, Ryn." He took my hand. "Let's help each other through the funeral, and then we'll talk."

In the end, we decided not to take Molly to the funeral. She stayed home with Lena, who was busy accepting food and flowers from the people who dropped by to pay their respects.

As Rosemary's only relatives, John and I sat together in the front row. I couldn't stop the tears from pouring down my face. Eventually he put his arm around me, pulled me against him, handed me his handkerchief and let me cry in his arms.

For the next few days, I felt hollow inside. Molly clung to me, and I had the feeling she was afraid I would go away too. John gave Lena some time off, so Molly and I baked cookies and made dinner every night, except for the one night I bought steaks for John to grill.

The three of us took walks in the woods and watched Abe, the trainer, work the horses in the ring.

One night John opened a bottle of good French wine. He raised a glass to me and said, "Cheers, Rynie. Here's to happier times!"

"John, I want happier times, but first, I want the truth about my sister."

"It will hurt you, Ryn. You don't want to know."

I had been thinking a lot about my sister the past week, and when I was being absolutely truthful with myself, I remembered not only her luminous moments, but also her dark side. "Rosemary cheated on you, didn't she?" I blurted it out. "If she hurt you, John, I'm so sorry, but I need the truth. Was it *your* baby she was carrying?"

"This is the really hard part, Ryn. I am pretty sure the baby was your husband Lawrence's."

Had I not been seated, I would have collapsed. As it was, the room began to spin and I spilled my wine on the glass cocktail table. "No!" I screamed as the red liquid spread like blood. "That's a lie! I don't believe you. That just can't be. Why would you lie to me?" I pounded my fists against his chest.

John grabbed my hands and held me. "Calm down, Ryn. You wanted the truth, and now you are going to hear it. I know you suspected I was in some way responsible for Rosemary's disappearance, and her suicide. You have always believed the worst of me, and I can't help that, but now I need you to listen...

"Rosemary and Lawrence fell in love in high school. She went away to college and Lawrence stayed in Lake James. They continued to date until they had a big fight. After that, Rosemary and I went out a few times. Then, all of a sudden she wanted to get married. It seemed sudden, but you know how alluring and convincing

45

Rosemary could be. So I believed she loved me, and we were wed. Not long after that, Lawrence married you."

Although I wanted to hide in shame, I could almost believe John's devastating words. I remembered how inseparable Rosemary and Lawrence had been, so that when they broke up and Lawrence married me, it had also seemed sudden, yet it was a little sister's dream come true. "But that was a long time ago," I weakly protested.

John let my hands go long enough to clean up the wine with his snow white handkerchief. He looked away, as though he felt shame, too. "I'm afraid our marriages didn't end the affair, Ryn. I discovered that Rosemary and Lawrence were meeting in a little cabin in Martinsville. In the meantime, my wife had been making excuses not to sleep with me. When she got pregnant the first time, I forced her to tell me the truth."

"You mean you are not Molly's father?"

"No, she is Lawrence's child, but I am the only father she has ever known. I love her like my own. I tried to keep us together for Molly's sake, but I warned Rosemary that if this ever happened again, I would file for divorce and get custody of Molly, claiming that she was an unfit mother.

"I hate to say it, but I believe it was Rosemary's intention to split the two of you up. Her phone records proved she had tried repeatedly to contact him. When Lawrence failed to respond, she became afraid, and was willing to do anything—even speak with you. But right after she wrote you that letter and before you came here,

Rosemary went to the Lake James Tribune, looking for answers. My theory is that when she found Lawrence's obituary, she panicked and drove her car into the lake."

John cradled me in his arms and let me cry for hours. Then he carried me to his bed and held me until I fell asleep. The next morning, he brought me a cup of coffee. He was followed by Molly dragging her favorite blanket and sucking her thumb.

"Rise and shine, Mate," he said. "We have an adventure planned today. Lena made breakfast for you. After you've eaten, come down to the stables. I want to show you something..."

John met me leading a filly with a shiny sable coat. "Abe just finished training this little beauty."

John showed me how to rub her nose. We allowed her an opportunity to see me and smell me, then he handed me an apple to feed her. Finally, he lifted me into the saddle and climbed up behind me.

I felt his warm breath on my neck, his black stubble against my cheek, and the goodness in his heart as our spirits united. I experienced an unexpected passion and desire for this man who pulled me against him, kicked the horse's flanks, and then made a clicking sound with his mouth. The little mare galloped as fast as she could, carrying us I knew not where. But as long as I was with John, I didn't care.

I never returned to Lake James. Several months later, John and I were married in St. Mark's Episcopal Church. Our love and passion only grew stronger through the joyous years. My handsome husband and I added three sons and another daughter to our family.

We made many trips to England, where I met my in-laws. Our fist son lives there now. Molly took over the antique shop, our second son is a horse trainer, and our youngest boy teaches history in a nearby college.

Our baby daughter, now in her early twenties, is a late bloomer. Actually, she's a spoiled Daddy's Girl. Last we heard, she was planning to become a veterinarian.

When we worry about her future, her father smiles at me and says, "Oh, not to worry Rynie, she'll be fine. She just needs to bugger about a bit."

SPECIAL DELIVERY

"The baby is coming!" my sister-in-law screamed. "Stop, pull over. Pull over now, Eric! Oh my God, hurry!"

The tires squealed and scratched across the gravel as I slammed on my breaks, put on my turn signals and pulled off the road. Fortunately, we were in a rural area with very little traffic. Unfortunately, I had no idea how in God's name to deliver a baby, but that's what I was about to do.

No time to call 911, no time for anything. I saw the terror on Casey's face as I grabbed her hand and helped her out of the car. There was blood on the car seat, on her dress and running down her legs. She took a few steps and fell to the ground.

I knelt down, lifted the blood- stained dress and saw a tiny head poking out between her legs. I had to push the grass back to get my hands under it. Then the chest appeared, and in a minute or two I held a baby boy in my trembling hands.

He was blue and slimy—covered with red goo. He looked up at me, took a deep breath and let out a blood-curdling scream. I handed him to Casey and made a mad dash to the trunk, where I kept a first aid kit. My clumsy fingers peeled off a strip of gauze and tied the umbilical cord.

When I drove up to the emergency entrance of the local hospital, I informed the nurses that I had just delivered my nephew, Terrance Alexander Stevens, Jr. I told them they would find him with his mother, outside in my car.

***

My sister-in-law Casey and I had been high school sweethearts and had dated through four years of college. Back then I worked in a pizza parlor to save enough money to buy her an engagement ring. I had enrolled in a Master's program hoping to go into research. Casey planned to work until we could afford to get married.

I thought my plans were all mapped out. I knew exactly how my future was going to unfold until my older brother Alex returned home after spending two years in the Navy.

Alex was handsome, outgoing and exciting. He loved beer, women, motorcycles, unfiltered Pal Malls and getting body tattoos.

I was just the opposite—nerdy, quiet, serious and studious. One of Alex's greatest pleasures in life was bullying, teasing and picking on me.

He knew exactly how to get under my skin, but flirting with my fiancé was a new low. He talked her into going for a thrill ride on his motorcycle, getting drunk and eloping. Then they moved in with Mom and Dad, leaving me devastated.

A few days after their marriage, they were on their way home from a bar when Alex drove head-on into a pickup truck.

They were both seriously injured. When Casey was well enough, Mom and Dad brought her home, but Alex's spinal cord had been severed. Our parents were inconsolable. Alex spent weeks in a rehab center, with Casey and Mom by his side, until arrangements could be made to bring him home with around-the-clock care. Our dining room was dismantled. A hospital bed and medical equipment were brought in.

I was so angry with Casey I could hardly control myself, and even madder when I learned that she was pregnant. It only made matters worse when I saw what the situation was doing to my parents. My father had a job to go to everyday. My mother was a strong woman, but she struggled under all the stress.

After the baby I delivered was born, I continued my graduate courses, but lived at home to help my family. My poor parents had one son who was unresponsive, in a vegetative state with nurses around the clock, a stressed-out daughter-in-law and a colicky grandson who cried all the time.

I found myself in the role of son, brother, brother- in- law and father to a baby boy whose mother I could barely stand. Casey had become a bitter complaining woman. She realized she had made a lot of mistakes and that life was passing her by.

In the meantime, I felt responsible for my nephew, little Terry. I rocked him when he was colicky. When he was older, I took him out for ice cream cones, fishing, camping—all those things his father couldn't do.

Eventually, I earned my degree and joined a team of clinical molecular geneticists. I analyzed research linked to abnormalities like familial cancer, cystic fibrosis, multiple dystrophy, Alzheimer's and other ailments.

A senior staff member introduced me to my teammates, who made me feel at home. On the second morning in my new job, a pretty doctor with brown hair and blue eyes came from the lab across the hall and said, "Welcome, Dr. Stevens. I thought you might like a hot cup of coffee." She placed two cups on my desk and pulled up a chair.

"Yes, thank you," I answered. "I remember you from yesterday. Dr. McDonald, isn't it?"

"It's Maril." She smiled.

Maril had been with the team for six months. Her blue eyes sparkled with excitement as she told me about her current project and the condo she was closing on in a few days. "Wait until I am all settled in, and then I'll invite you over to see it," she promised.

From that moment on, Maril McDonald took me under her wing as she would an injured bird. She collected art, so I volunteered to hang the paintings in her new home.

She cooked wonderful meals for me. We talked for hours by candlelight and drank imported wine until well into the night.

By Christmas I had moved in with her. We bought a tree and decorated it with ornaments she had bought in England. We made a wonderful turkey dinner together, exchanged presents and were watching a football game when I got a call from Mama. Alex was dead.

After the funeral, I brought my nephew Terry home with me. The three of us went on vacation until after New Year's. Maril and I treated Terry to movies, sightseeing trips and anything to get his mind off his father. He was eight years old at the time.

Six months after Alex died, Casey remarried. Evidently, she and her boyfriend had been eagerly waiting for her to be free. She took Terry away from us to live with her and her new husband. Sharing my nephew with a stepfather made me very uncomfortable, so I bought Terry a cell phone and told him to call me anytime he needed me.

Maril and I were married by the time Terry graduated from High School. I had gotten back in Casey's good graces by agreeing to pay for his college. Our lab was affiliated with an outstanding Ivy League school, where I was able to get Terry a scholarship and enroll him in a computer science program.

He adjusted quickly to his studies, and one afternoon he rode his bike over to our laboratory. I gave him my usual bear hug and explained the project I was working on. Then I said, "Go across the hall and say hello to Aunt Maril before you go."

Later that afternoon, Maril came over to see me. "Eric, Terry is interested in researching his ancestors. He wants to know all about the Stevens family, so I took his DNA sample. I need to get yours too, so we can find out exactly who you guys are."

A couple of weeks later, my wife was all excited when she showed up at my desk. "Eric, can you come across the hall? I have something amazing to show you.

"I have the ancestry information about your family," she continued, "but the astonishing part is what I discovered in the DNA. Eric, I can say without a doubt that Terry is *not* your nephew."

"Well, of course he is. I delivered him myself by the side of the road—in the grass."

A big grin spread across Maril's face. "No, Eric, you delivered your own son—yours and Casey's. Terry's genetic code and yours are the same. Your chromosome copy is identical. There is absolutely no doubt, Eric."

Maril put her arms around me and kissed the tears rolling down my cheeks. "How wonderful is that?"

"Too good to be true!" I finally managed to exclaim. "I don't know how to tell Terry, though. I don't know what he'll think," I stammered. "He'll have a million questions, but I don't know how to answer them yet. How do we break that kind of news?"

"Oh, Eric, he'll be so happy! You are the only father he has ever known. Let's invite him for dinner. We'll cook his favorite meal, and when the time is right, you'll simply tell him you love him."

That special night I grilled steaks and baked potatoes on the grill and the three of us ate on the deck. It was a warm summer evening. Fireflies twinkled in and out of the crape myrtle trees alongside our balcony.

Eventually Maril excused herself to make coffee and serve the cake. It was Terry's favorite chocolate pound cake with a scoop of vanilla ice cream on top.

After she returned with the cake and passed out the plates, Terry added cream and sugar to his coffee and stirred. "By the way, Aunt Maril, did you ever get the results from my DNA test?"

"Yes I did, Terry. Would you like to know what it showed?"

"Did it prove that my ancestors were British?"

"Yes."

"Did it show that my fifth great grandfather was old what's-his-name Stevens from Devonshire?"

"Actually, his name was William Arthur Stevens from Yorkshire."

Terry laughed and stuffed a huge bite of cake in his mouth. He was trying to chew and talk at the same time when he said, "I hope it showed that the famous British musician, Yusuf Islam, otherwise known as Cat Stevens, was a distant cousin. That would be way cool."

"Sorry, to disappoint you," Maril chuckled. "You are not related to Cat Stevens nor to the royal family, but I did find one thing of interest..." She paused, cleared her throat and said. "Alex Stevens was not your father, but Eric is."

Terry sat motionless, as if he were in shock. He blinked and then stared up at the stars twinkling above the campus. Eventually, he smiled and placed his arm on the back of Eric's chair. Neither man spoke. There was no need. The two had bonded years ago, probably by the side of the road when Eric's shaking hands cut the umbilical cord and held the screaming baby against his heart.

DADDY'S GIRL

My hair was still wet from the shower when I heard Beau arrive unexpectedly and yell my name. "I'm upstairs, come on up!" I hollered.

"I have someone with me."

"Okay, I'll be right down."

Beau was seated on the sofa across the room from a teenage girl. As soon as I walked in I felt the anger and hostility stretching across the room from one to the other.

Beau looked like he had been sucking on a lemon and the girl looked mad enough to strangle him. My little poodle, Doodle, was in the girl's lap licking her mouth, probably enjoying the juice from the pink bubblegum she was smacking. The girl wore a threadbare pair of jeans, a tank top with *peace* written across it and a pair of red tennis shoes with holes in the toes. Her untamed black hair made her look like a character from *Wild Thing*.

"Mia, this is my daughter, Jody," Beau announced.

"Your daughter!" I said as I fell into the nearest chair.

Beau is a writer. He has published a number of novels that have made him famous, wealthy, and a little arrogant. We grew up next door to each other and have been together off and on all of our lives. Our parents always thought we would marry. It's not that he never asked me—it's that I always said no.

Every eligible woman in town wanted to marry Beau McFadden. His black curly hair, baby blue eyes and soft voice were mesmerizing. He could sweep a woman off her feet in a heartbeat, and God knows these women tried to catch him, but none could make him happy.

I love him. I would do anything for him. But I will not let him break my heart. His latest bimbo is a cute, empty headed little thing named Sienna. What the hell kind of name is Sienna?

I was in a state of shock, waiting for somebody to say something, when the girl rolled her eyes and faced me. "Well since my old man doesn't know his ass from a hole in the ground, I'll bring you up to speed, lady.

"When he and Mom were in college, they got drunk as skunks at a school frat party, and I'm the result. Mom didn't like him well enough to have a baby with him, so she never told him she was pregnant.

"Between her boyfriends and her drugs, I had to learn to take care of myself. After Mom died from an overdose, I found a letter telling me that if anything happened to her, I should go live with *him*," she finished petulantly.

Beau was about to explode. When he got nervous, he fidgeted—crossing and uncrossing his legs. "Jody showed up at my parent's house, so Mom and Dad took her to Sienna's," he explained.

Jody looked at me and yelled, "Yeah, and I won't spend another friggin' minute with that damn bitch, and I'm sure not gonna live with this fuck-up."

"Mom and Dad are busy with their book store," Beau whined. "They're too old to have a teenager in the house, but Jody and I have done nothing but butt heads all week. It's obvious we can't live together."

Gradually it dawned on me that Beau hadn't come here simply to introduce me to his daughter. And although it was hard to imagine Beau as a father, when I looked at Jody's curly black hair and baby blue eyes, I had absolutely no doubt that she was his.

"It would just be for a short time, Mia, long enough for me to find a suitable boarding school," he pleaded.

Jody rolled her eyes again and shouted, "I've already told you, old man, I'm not going to a stupid boarding school. I've lived in roach- infested apartments, on the street, and in a homeless shelter. I can damn well do it again."

"You'll have to excuse your father," I intervened. "I'm sure he wants to keep you. He just doesn't know how to be a dad *yet*. Don't worry, we'll work this out. I'd like you to stay with me, Jody. I see you brought your suitcase, so follow me upstairs and I'll show you your room."

Then I turned to Beau and whispered harshly, "Don't you dare go anywhere. We need to talk."

Clearly the girl had really gotten his goat. He sighed and said, "God damn it!'" under his breath. In the meantime, Jody picked up her suitcase with one hand and gave him the finger with the other before following me upstairs, with my happy little poodle trailing right behind.

I happen to be a guidance counselor in the local junior high school, so I deal with teenagers every day. Thank goodness we were on summer vacation, so I had time to spend with this little girl who needed all the help she could get.

I warned Beau to stay away until both his and Jody's tempers had cooled off. After he left, I went up to check on her. She was sitting on the bed with Doodle, who was licking the tears streaming down her cheeks. I put my arms around her and held her close. "Jody, I know this is very hard for you. You must miss your mother terribly. What was her name?"

"Kate," she said, holding back tears and trying to be brave.

"Jody, I know your father. He is a good man. If he had known about you, things would have been very different."

When Jody finally woke up the next morning, she told me she didn't eat breakfast, but I talked her into trying a cup of my hazelnut coffee before we headed downtown. After she finished her coffee, we went to *Fergie's* and bought some shorts, tee shirts, and a pair of sandals.

When I was standing at the cash register, I looked around and saw Jody hugging a teddy bear. "Would you like to take him home?"

She was on the verge of tears when she said, "No, that's okay."

I handed the bear to the cashier and added it to my purchases.

"You didn't have to do that," Jody said as we walked down the street to a little café.

"I know," I said. "What shall we call him?"

"It's a *her,* and I want to call her Kate—for my mother."

"What a great idea! I'd like you tell me all about Kate."

I handed Jody a menu and asked her what she felt like eating.

"I always get a hamburger and fries."

"Let's try something different," I suggested, and ordered fried shrimp, hushpuppies, slaw, sweet tea and peach ice cream.

Later, we visited a music store, bought some C D's and a poster of her favorite band. That afternoon I helped her fix up her room. We brought up a bookcase from downstairs and a stereo that I wasn't using. We made a music center and hung her new poster above it. I learned her favorite color was yellow and promised to buy a yellow bedspread.

Jody placed Kate on her bed next to the spot Doodle had claimed for himself. Her body seemed to relax as she looked around her room—her safe place. "I've never had my own room," she confessed.

Soon we drove around town, so I could show her the school she would attend. I also pointed out the library, city park, movie theater and other places of interest.

It just so happened that Beau's best friend, Dick Martin, lived down the street from me. His daughter, Julie, was the same age as Jody. After I introduced the two girls, they became buddies and began hanging out together.

Three days a week I worked out at the Y. I took Jody along and enrolled her in a swim class, only to learn that she was already an experienced swimmer. Her instructor convinced her to join the swim team.

We visited her paternal grandparents, Lenore and Louis, at the McFadden Book Store, where Beaus' latest book was displayed in the window. Jody was reading the blurb inside the cover when Lenore said, "Jody, your dad's fortieth birthday is next Saturday. We plan to celebrate with a cookout in the backyard, and we want you and Mia to come."

Jody had a surprised look on her face. "Wow, next Saturday is my birthday, too!"

"Oh, my goodness!" squealed Lenore as she hugged her granddaughter. "We're going to have a wonderful party, and you'll get to meet the rest of your family."

Beau had followed my instructions to stay away, but word got around that his daughter was on the swim team and curiosity got the better of him. One night at a swim meet, Beau walked in and sat on the bleachers beside me.

"Well, look what the cat dragged in!" I said.

My body tingled all over when he sat beside me, and our legs touched. Between the noisy kids and the splashing water, I barely heard him when he leaned against me and said, "I broke up with Sienna. I'm living back at my house now."

Just then the girl's team burst from the locker room, and each child was introduced as she entered the pool area. I felt Beau's body tense when Jody appeared. Her black curly hair framed her bright blue eyes—the same blue as her Y swim suit. Beau didn't move a muscle as the announcer called her name:

"In lane four—Jody McFadden!"

"You got her hair cut?" he asked. Then before Jody sat down to wait her turn, a boy ran over and patted her on the back. "Who the hell is he?" Beau asked.

"Oh, that's Will. He's kind of a boyfriend, I think."

"What does that mean, *kind of* a boyfriend? She's way too young to have a boyfriend."

"Beau, she'll be fifteen on Saturday. I had a boyfriend at fifteen. Remember?"

"You mean that jerk, Alex? That pimply-faced loser you had the hots for?"

"That's the one." I smiled.

"Oh, Christ," he replied.

Jody was in the first event—freestyle. When the whistle blew, the girls dove in and headed down the lane. The noise was deafening. Beau was tense as he watched her turn the first lap and head back down the lane, turn again and go for the last lap. All the parents were yelling, but none were louder than Beau and me as we watched our girl come in third.

Before the backstroke event, Jody was standing in the pool waiting for the starting whistle. When it sounded, she pushed off with her feet and jettisoned herself down the lane ahead of all the others. She raised one arm above her head as the other arm swept beside her hip. Her feet fluttered as she reversed her arms and gracefully swam to the end of the pool, where she put her feet against the wall and flipped. The applause grew louder and cheers reverberated off the ceiling. Beau and I yelled at the top of our lungs, "Go Jody!" She made the last turn, put her feet against the wall, flipped and headed to finish first.

Beau had yelled until he was out of breath. He was shaking with excitement when he grabbed my hand and hugged me.

Afterwards, we stood with the parents congregating outside the locker room door. Beau beamed with pride as people congratulated him, while I waited to see how his daughter would respond when she saw him. Silently I prayed, *Please Jody, don't say anything embarrassing.*

But unfortunately when Beau called out, "Good job Jody!" she just turned her back on him and headed to the car.

"She'll come around," I told him hopefully.

The day of their joint birthdays, Jody wore her yellow shorts to show off her tan and talked me into letting her wear light pink lipstick to the party.

"Sweetie," I said, "This is your Dad's fortieth birthday. I know you've heard the saying 'over the hill,' so this is not the best time to call him 'my old man'. 'Asshole' would not be good, and neither would 'fuck-up'. Do you understand?"

She rolled her baby blue eyes, gave me a little peck on the cheek and said, "Yo, you got it, Mama Mia."

Jody's Grandma Lenore had tied birthday balloons on two chairs for the honorees, at a table laden with presents and a cake bearing the words "Happy Birthday, Jody and Beau."

My neighbors, Dick and Julie Martin, brought their daughter, Julie, Jody's new best friend. And Jody's aunts, uncles, and cousins were all eager to meet Beau's mystery child.

Jody opened her gifts first, leaving the smallest package until last. It was Beau's, beautifully wrapped in pink paper and tied with a silver ribbon. She unwrapped the package and pulled out a cell phone.

I held my breath, wondering what she would say. When she glanced in my direction, I saw tears in her eyes.

I winked at her as she put her arms around Beaus' neck, and barely above a whisper, I heard her say, "Thank you Daddy!"

Later, Beau sat on a bench beside her and helped her program numbers into the new phone.

"Beau," Dick said, "let's you and me take the girls sailing tomorrow. I'll get Janice to pack a picnic and we'll spend the day on the lake."

The next day, I couldn't wait for Jody to return from the father/daughter sailing adventure. I hoped that she and Beau had at least been civil to one another.

Before they left, Jody had said, "Mama Mia, I want a bikini like Julie's. My old, uh, my *daddy* heard me tell Julie that I was gonna ask you for one, then he got all cranked up and said, *You can't have a bikini!* That proves he doesn't give a damn about me."

"That's not true," I told her. "He's just very protective. That's a sign that he loves you."

"Yeah, right!" She scoffed.

"Okay, I'll have a talk with him."

A few days later, we found a cute bikini at *Fergie's*. We got Jody's ears pierced and bought a pair of tiny silver earrings.

Soon Beau began showing up at every swim meet with a cooler of Gatorade, a bag of energy snacks and a camera hung around his neck.

One night we were all in Beaus' convertible, on our way to a swim meet in a nearby town, when Jody said, "Daddy, I'll have my learner's permit before long. Will you let me drive your car?"

He groaned, "We'll see."

After that meet, we were waiting outside the locker room when I slipped on a wet spot, thrust out my right arm trying to break the fall, and felt it snap.

Beau and Jody helped me to the car, then rushed me to the emergency room. I came home in a cast, with pain pills to take every four hours and instructions to rest— no kitchen duty and no showers.

Beau helped me into bed, gave me a pain pill, kissed me and said, "Thank you for being a good mother to my daughter."

He spent the night in the spare bedroom. The next morning, he and Jody made my breakfast, brought it up to my room and took turns feeding me. We all had a cup of hazelnut coffee—Jody's piled high with all the Reddi Whip she could squirt on top.

The following week, Beau got a six figure advance for his next book and was given a deadline to meet. In order to spend more time with his daughter and help me through my convalescence, he moved most of his things into my spare bedroom and created an office in a little nook at the end of the hall.

One morning after Beau and Jody put the breakfast dishes in the dishwasher, he went to his office and began working on the computer. I was in bed watching TV, when

Jody crawled in beside me. I had been watching the movie *Finding Nemo*. Marlin's son, Nemo, had just freed a school of fish from a net, when Nemo got knocked unconscious and lay at the bottom of the ocean. Marlin panicked and tried to rescue his son. "Nemo, Nemo!" he cried, "It's okay, Daddy's here! Daddy's got you!"

Jody and I were sobbing our eyes out when Beau stuck his head in the door and asked, "Can I get you two anything, maybe a box of Kleenex?"

Several nights later, about 2AM, we were all startled awake by wind blasting the house, torrential rain and hail clattering against the windows. Tree limbs hit the roof and streaks of lightning flashed through the sky. Jody climbed in bed with me, and Doodle dove under our covers.

A flash of lightening silhouetted Beau in the doorway. "The power's out. Are you okay, Jody?"

"No, I'm scared to death!" she shrieked.

"This is just an ordinary summer storm, honey," he said in soothing tones. "We have them all the time here. It'll be over soon, but I'll stay close until it stops."

Beau lay down beside me, and before long, his body relaxed and his breathing grew heavier. Soon it was punctuated with soft little snores. As soon as the storm was over, Jody picked up Doodle and headed for her room. I moved over to give Beau more space, but he just moved closer and snored in my ear.

I loved having Beau and Jody taking care of me, but my cast was coming off soon and I didn't know what would happen then. Would Beau move back home? He and Jody had gotten to know each other and even showed signs of affection. Our lives together seemed so normal.

One night they were cleaning up after dinner when the doorbell rang, and Jody went to answer it.

"Daddy, there's a man here who says he's here about the pool you're gonna build in the backyard!"

When Beau returned from speaking with the man, Jody said, "Daddy, help me get this straight. This is Mama Mia's house and her backyard, but you plan to build a pool in it?"

Beau fidgeted. He crossed and uncrossed his legs.

"Yeah, Beau, I'm trying to get this straight, too," I said. "A pool in *my* backyard?"

"I only asked the man for an estimate," he said.

Jody spoke up, "Daddy, you two already act like an old married couple. I know you've been sleeping together. Next thing you'll tell me is I'll be getting a little brother or sister. What will people think?"

Beau blushed, shrugged his shoulders and offered a sheepish grin

"Daddy, this isn't funny. It's time you two got married! Mia loves you."

"I know she loves me, Jody, but after all, Mia's a strong woman with a mind of her own. If we got married, I expect our babies would be just like her. Oh, by the way,

69

did I mention that I put my house on the market and it's under contract?"

I didn't know whether to laugh or cry, but I put my good arm around Beau and kissed him. We were locked in a clumsy embrace, when Jody's phone rang.

"Yo, Will," she said to the phone. "Yeah, I can talk as soon as I get away from these two disgusting wackos pretending to be my parents." She turned and headed up the stairs, with a fuzzy little dog at her heels.

Soon after that, I had a serious talk with Beau about how important it is for girls to grow up to be strong, independent women. I told him that fathers could empower their daughters by showing confidence in their abilities.

He laughed. "Well, hell, I don't want any daughter of mine to grow up *un-empowered.*"

Beau had a trip planned to New York to meet with his publisher. I suggested it would be a wonderful experience for Jody if he took her along. So on a bright sunny morning, the two of them boarded a plane for the Big Apple. Jody sat by the window and watched in wonder as her town became a tiny speck and then disappeared beneath the clouds.

Beau booked a room in one of New York's best hotels. He took Jody along to meet his publisher. They went on a sightseeing tour, and one night as they were dining in one of New York's best restaurants, he handed her two tickets to *The Lion King.*

Jody McFadden came home wearing a *Lion King* tee shirt. She was so excited, I thought she would never settle down. She had a new poster for her room and a soundtrack CD that she played continuously.

The contractor came to our door when construction of the pool was nearly complete. Jody answered and called out, "Daddy, the man wants to talk to you about which kind of diving board to install."

"You talk to him, Jody," Beau said. "You make that decision."

"Okay!" she exclaimed, her voice filled with pride.

We watched out the window as she led the man to the far end of the pool. He bent down and pointed, then stood up and handed her some sample photos. She looked at each one carefully before she chose one and handed it to him.

"Looks like Jody's empowered." Beau smiled and wrapped his arm around me.

And as I looked across the yard, I could almost hear the laughter of all the kids who would someday swim in that pool. They would drink pitchers of pink and purple Kool-Ade and eat the mountains of hot dogs and hamburgers Beau would grill.

Suddenly, I felt a fierce kick in my side from the son we were expecting. Beau pointed to a spot beside the driveway. "Don't you think that's a good place for the basketball goal?"

"It's perfect," I agreed.

JENNY'S SECRET LOVE

We had him cremated. He was only fifty five. A rare form of cancer and liver damage from alcohol abuse ate away at him until there was nothing left but a pile of bones. I thought he would live forever just to prolong our misery, but Fate intervened.

Through the years, he beat the mortal hell out of my mother and me. His hateful words are forever branded in my memory and burned into my soul. He showed no gratitude or remorse in his last days when we tried to care for him and ease his pain.

We didn't have a funeral. His ashes were put in a bronze urn. Mama refused to bring it into the house, so I took it to the barn and buried it in a horse stall.

I don't remember much about my childhood. Mostly I recall the old man didn't love me, or anybody else for that matter. It's a miracle I didn't kill him. I knew where he kept his gun, and God knows I was tempted, but again, Fate took care of it. Good thing, because the bloody old fart wasn't worth my spending time in jail or burning in hell.

He was a father you didn't disagree with. Even his words landed like a fist. Our lives consisted of one dreary day after another, and I tried hard not to remember any of them.

We were like inmates confined to the same prison cell, hoping to find a way to escape, knowing damned well we had received a life sentence.

My mama and Troy Thompson eloped when she was 18 and he was 19. She knew soon enough she'd made a horrible mistake. He would get drunk and throw the king of fits.

Mama started going to the Catholic Church to find solace. When she asked Father Angus MacKenzie to hear her confession, she sat on a chair and peered through the little lattice window at the man on the other side. The priest was a tall, handsome red haired man with a soft voice, blue eyes and a heavy Scottish accent. She kept going back because Father MacKenzie always ended by saying, "Will ya not come again soon, Jenny?" It was mathematically impossible for her to sin enough to need three confessions a week, but seeing the handsome, soft spoken priest through the little latticed window made her happier than she had ever been in her life.

One day she was late. Angus MacKenzie was waiting. When he opened the little window of the confessional and saw her black eye and the bruises on her face, he stormed out of the booth, grabbed her by the hand, led her into his office, and eventually took her to his apartment to tend to her wounds.

Mama stopped going to confessional, but she did not stop her secret love affair with the Catholic priest until she started showing.

Angus had sinned against his church, his God and everything the Catholic Church believed in. He left the church and became a teacher in the local high school. I had him for history my senior year. He entered the class room every morning, brushed his curly red hair away from his face and greeted us with a hearty Gaelic, "Maidin mhaith, lads and lassies."

He published several books about Scotland and his ancestors, who immigrated to North Carolina in the 1700's. He was proud of his heritage and the fact that his people fought in our American Revolution for independence. He talked often about his great - great grandfather, who grew up in the Highlands. The Scots loved to tell stories, and Clan MacKenzie was no exception. They passed tall tales down from generation to generation.

All my life I had worried about my future—mostly about becoming a sorry alcoholic like my old man. I was downright scared when I learned that alcoholism was an inherited disease, so I decided to live the life of a monk. By damn, I was never going to become the kind of man who beat his wife and children.

Girls were attracted to me, and my hormones raged from the tenth grade on, but I kept my distance, never once asking a girl out.

Troy Thomson died a couple of months before my graduation. I got a job in a farm supply store to help support Mama, but one week before I was scheduled to start, a letter came from North Carolina State University saying that I had been given a full scholarship by an anonymous donor.

I showed it to Mama, who didn't seem at all surprised. She just smiled and said, "Well, I guess you'll be needin' some new clothes, Colin."

When I argued that she needed me to work and help out at home, she laughed. "I'm planning to sell the farm, then buy a house in town and a new car to park in the driveway."

Mama had become a nurse after I started first grade and worked in a nearby hospital. "We'll make out just fine," she said. "And besides, I got a nice check from Troy's insurance, you received that scholarship, so you're definitely going to college."

I loved college and made good grades. My advisor, Mr. Cates, gave me a lot of encouragement and helped me decide to major in history.

It was in Mr. Cates class that I met Beth, who drew me like a magnet. Must have been that darn Fate thing again. When that girl smiled at me, I just lost it—first my self- discipline, and then my virginity.

Just before the Christmas holidays, our history professor gave us an assignment to research our family origins, including a timeline showing where our ancestors came from and how they contributed to the foundation of this country. We were to use old photos, letters, anything we could find.

With thoughts of Beth and her sweet kisses still on my mind, I wondered how in the world I could turn in a paper about the sorry Thompson family. I would die of humiliation.

As soon as I got home, I began my assignment. Mama agreed to help me. We started with her family. That was pretty easy, but then I started on the Thompsons. I dug out old photo albums, visited graveyards and went to the Registrar of Deeds. No one had anything good to say about my father's family. Mama knew how embarrassed I would be to put this scandalous stuff on paper and give it to my professor.

"Mama," I said, "My daddy's ashes are buried under a pile of horse shit, my granddaddy died in prison, my grandma suffers from screaming fits and my only living uncle's in the nuthouse."

Then Mama started crying and said, "Stop it, Colin, this is so wrong and I can't live with this lie anymore."

She ran into her bedroom and slammed the door. I could hear her crying and talking on the phone to someone. She didn't come out until the next morning, when she said, "I'm sorry Colin, but it's time you heard the truth, and you are going to hear it today."

At mid- morning the doorbell rang and I went to answer it. There stood Angus MacKenzie, his copper-colored hair lit on fire by the morning sun, the same as my own.

He regarded me with a slow, wide smile and swallowed hard trying to hide his nervousness. His Adam's apple moved up and down his freshly shaved neck as he searched for words. His blue eyes filled with tears when he said, "I have loved you since the day you were born, son."

Mama held Angus' face between her hands and kissed him on the mouth. He brushed his hand across her cheek and said, "I love you, Mo Ghraidh."

My legs buckled. I collapsed in a chair and waited for somebody to say something. Angus MacKenzie spoke first, rolling rrr's around in his mouth like he was choking. Then Mama said, "You better let *me* tell him, Angus."

I sat frozen in suspense as she revealed to me their secret love affair and the father I never knew I had.

The minute I returned to school, I invited Beth to meet me for pizza and a beer at a deli where students hung out.

When she arrived in jeans and a tight- fitting red sweater, blond hair cascading over her shoulders, I threw my arms around her and kissed her. The room erupted with cheering. Beer glasses were raised by students still giddy with holiday spirit.

Well, I was giddy too, and I hadn't even had a drink. Beth and I settled in a booth and ordered beer. Soon I was feeling no pain and still fuzzy about who the hell I was anyway when I heard a voice in my head and an image flashed before me: William Jonathan Alistair

Hamish Mackenzie in his kilt. He was standing in front of a fireplace, his pewter mug raised to me as he said, "Slainte, my lad, it's your old kinsman here. It's my blood you have. You do me proud. Gus math a theid leat to you laddie."

The next day I turned in my assignment. It contained information about my great-great-great grandfather's arrival in Philadelphia in 1743 and a picture of him in his clan plaid, holding his sword. I had legal documents showing that he fought in the American Revolution and papers detailing my great grandfather's time served in the Civil War. I included pictures of my grandparents and one of my father, a little red headed boy surrounded by his four brothers and two sisters—my uncles and aunts. I also had a copy of a document from my father's lawyer stating that my name had been changed to William Colin Angus Mackenzie.

My father married my mother on New Year's Eve of that year. Because, he said, he meant to start the New Year off right. James William Angus Mackenzie was truly an honorable man. I got to know and love him well. He gave me life, his blood, his family, his name and the clan MacKenzie, whose motto was: *Loyal to the end.*

Gene Pool

His little brown body came running from the edge of the water, slinging sand all over my blanket. "Mama, I'm hungry."

"So am I, Nick, but I have to get you dry first." I wrapped my beach towel around him, then covered him with sun screen, unwrapped some sandwiches and poured two cups of lemonade.

I tried to find a position in my folding chair that would satisfy the baby I was expecting. In a few minutes, it stopped kicking and I was comfortable. I sat listening to the waves crashing on the beach and thinking about how Peter and I met and started our family.

****

Harrison J. Sims III, my first husband, a prominent attorney from an old Charleston family, expected me to produce Harrison J. Sims IV. The Sims behaved like they were descendants of Henry VIII, still carrying his genes and his mind set. After three years of marriage, when I still had not produced a male child or any child, they wanted to chop my head off.

We lived in an old historic section near the Battery in a big house surrounded by palm trees. I drove a BMW, wore the latest fashions and dined in the finest restaurants. In fact, I had everything except a male heir to the Sims' throne.

Harry and I had spent a fortune on doctors and fertility clinics. He was a very methodical man. We had sex only when my calendar and temperature charts indicated I might be fertile. I had run out of options except one—artificial insemination. I would give Harry Sims a son and no one would ever know my secret.

My appointment was on a Wednesday morning at 11:30. Only one other person was in the waiting room of the clinic when I arrived: a young man dressed in a plaid shirt and khaki shorts. He had a pleasant face, dark curly hair and big brown eyes. The Charleston sun had turned his lean, muscular body a golden tan. He was in his late twenties or early thirties and appeared to be as nervous as I was.

I tried to calm myself by watching his strong calf muscles and his big feet and long brown toes in navy flip flops that made a swish, swish sound as he paced back and forth in front of me. Finally, he stopped and sat in the chair next to me, accidently bumping my elbow.

"Sorry," he said.

Soon a woman appeared and spoke to him, "Sir, there's been a misunderstanding, your appointment isn't until next week."

He looked frustrated and disappointed as he got up and headed for the door, and I did something totally out of character for my prim and proper Charlestonian life style—I got up and followed him.

He went into a deli about a block away and had just ordered lunch when I approached him. "May, I join you?" I asked. He pulled out a chair and motioned for me to have a seat.

"You were in the clinic!" he said.

"Yes," I replied.

"You followed me, why?"

"I'm not sure. I heard a little voice in my head, intuition, my inner spirit, maybe, telling me that I should talk to you."

"I don't believe in spirits, but I'm listening, so please go ahead and talk."

"Well, maybe we could make an arrangement, the two of us."

"You want to get pregnant, right?"

"Yes."

"Make me an offer." He smiled and shook his head.

"I'll pay you three hundred dollars each time we meet, and if I get pregnant, I'll pay you ten thousand."

"Well, that's very generous, and I do have a lot of student loans and other bills. That's way more than the clinic pays, but wouldn't it be easier for you to get it done there?"

"Yes—maybe, but I need to see a real person, a face to remember not just someone in a white coat inserting a rod between my legs. You look like someone I could trust."

"This is crazy. You do know that, don't you?" Clearly the handsome young man had never expected such a bizarre proposal, but eventually he agreed to my offer.

He wrote his address and telephone number on a napkin and handed it to me. "I am a senior in college. I have Monday and Wednesday mornings free, also Tuesday and Thursday afternoons. You choose."

"I will be there tomorrow afternoon at 4:00." We shook hands and said goodbye.

His name was Peter Nicholas Latham. He lived in a second story one room studio right off the campus. I climbed the stairs and knocked on his door. When he answered he was barefoot, wearing shorts and a college T- shirt. His dark curly hair was still wet from the shower and I could smell his shampoo.

"I'm really nervous," he confessed. "I need a glass of wine to loosen up, or I'm not sure I can perform."

He poured two glasses and handed me one. I sat on the side of his bed and drank my wine. I stared at his desk across the room. It was piled with books and a computer showing an unfinished paper he had been working on. I smelled something cooking and heard muffled voices coming from next door.

"You have a husband?" Peter asked.

"Yes."

"Does he know you're doing this?"

"He'll never know," I answered with finality.

He turned away from me and wiped perspiration from his brow with the back of his hand.

After a few minutes, I took off my clothes and pulled the sheet up over me. I could feel my cheeks burning from embarrassment.

Eventually he joined me. Our coupling was quick and over before I knew it. I gave him the money and said I would call him call again.

When I called, I realized that he'd never even asked my name. Would he know who I was? The phone rang three times before he answered. "This is Karen," I gulped.

"Oh, it's *you*," he said without hesitation. "Okay, when do you want to come again?"

This time he answered the door after my first knock. "Karen, is it? What's your last name?"

"Sims," I said, "Karen Sims."

He immediately uncorked a bottle of red wine, poured two glasses and chattered a bit, trying to relax. "I have a big exam tomorrow," he said, "I need to study when we are done here."

"Do you have a girlfriend?"

"Not one that matters."

He moved to the side of the bed near the window and removed his clothes. I did the same, covering myself with the sheet.

"This might be a mistake," I stammered. "Maybe we should call off our—I started to say "arrangement," but it was too late. He meant to be gentle, but his hands trembled and he breathed deeply as he lifted the sheet and found me. It took longer than before. Afterwards I raised my legs and lay still to be sure the semen had a chance to reach its destination. Finally I placed three hundred dollar bills on his desk and left.

Harry was in New York at a conference when I next met Peter. I told him we could take our time, and that I didn't have to hurry home.

So we drank two glasses of wine before he unbuttoned my blouse and unfastened my bra. "We don't have to rush? Good."

I felt his warm breath on my stomach as he lowered me gently down on the bed, then leaned forward on his elbows to kiss me. He took his time and it was amazing. Afterwards he lay down beside me and held my hand.

Neither of us said anything for quite a while, until he announced that he was going down to the deli and asked what he could bring me.

When he returned, we sat up in bed, ate corned beef on rye, potato chips, drank beer and laughed like a couple of teenagers.

Peter brushed crumbs off my lips and kissed me. "Isn't this is a lot more fun than having some strange dude put a rod between your legs?"

I smiled at him. I didn't have to say anything. He knew how I felt.

Next time I visited Peter, I had missed a period. I told him I might be pregnant, but wouldn't know for another month.

"Then, you can throw away the thermometer and the charts?"

"I think so."

I never expected the wave of sadness that swept over me after that. I would truly miss him, his laughter, his big bare feet and long toes as he tiptoed around in his little studio apartment. Sometimes he was naked, sometimes we both were. We were happy.

The doctor confirmed my pregnancy after I missed the second period, so I withdrew ten thousand from my checking account and went to give Peter the news.

Harry was out of town again, so I told Peter that I was in no hurry to get home.

"Then please don't go," he said gently. "This might be our last time together. Stay with me."

He made our dinner using his hot plate and toaster oven, and then he studied while I read one of the mystery novels he had collected. It was almost midnight when he came to bed and we made love for the second time. His soft lips brushed mine and his words were no more than a whisper when he murmured into my hair, "I love you, Karen."

He tried not to wake me, but I felt him rise and go to the window. He stood there, tall and naked. "Are you all right?" I asked.

"I can't sleep."

I went to him, put my arm around his waist and together we watched the traffic on the street below. He put his hand on my stomach and said, "Will you let me see the baby when it's born?"

I kissed him and led him back to bed. "I am so sorry, Peter. We've been living a big lie, and it's all my fault. I have hurt you, our baby, and I've been unfaithful to my husband." Tears streamed down my cheeks.

"Karen, I have nothing to offer you or this baby. You did this for Harry and *your* family. He can offer the child a better life than I can. Maybe our baby will sit on the Sim's throne and inherit a fortune. I knew what I was getting into when I agreed to this arrangement. Don't worry, when you have this baby and get back to your family, you will forget me."

"I will never forget you. You *are* my family. Every time I look at this child, I will think of you and I will want you."

After we parted, we often talked on the phone and saw each other frequently. Peter graduated, got a good job, rented a larger apartment and gave me a key. *Just in case you need it,* he said.

My labor pains started early on a Monday morning. Harry kept up a constant nervous chatter on our drive to the hospital. It was nearly four hours before they wheeled me into the delivery room, leaving him to wait down the hall.

It's hard to remember much after that except trying to follow my instructions to *push harder, that's it, keep going, you're doing great, you're almost there, there it comes, it's here!*

A long silence followed and I started to worry until suddenly I heard a shrill scream that only a newborn can make. I remember lifting my head trying to see my baby, but instead I saw Dr. Benson and the concerned look on his face.

He and the nurses were whispering as though there was something they didn't want me to hear, but I did hear: *Yes, he will lighten up in time, but look at the color of his genitals. That's always a sure sign.*

Finally, Dr. Benson brought the baby and laid him on my breast. You have a fine son Mrs. Sims. I am going to speak to your husband, then I will talk to both of you in your room.

The baby looked very dark. I could have sworn he belonged to someone else, but *I* had just delivered him. He was mine. I uncovered his feet. He had big feet and long toes. He opened his eyes and looked at me. I knew he wanted me to nurse him and to love him. It was at that moment I knew I would love him more than life itself.

I also knew that Harry Sims was no fool, and I would have some explaining to do.

When I arrived in my room, Dr. Benson was not far behind. "Your husband has left the hospital," he said. "We had a long talk and I explained to him that sometimes a recessive gene shows up. This child may have inherited a recessive African American gene. Mr. Sims was extremely upset and said the Sims do not harbor African American genes and that you will not insult them by bringing this little bastard into his house."

Somehow I managed to call Peter at his job and told him what had happened.

"God, I am so sorry, Karen. Your husband is a four-star fool. I'm sending a friend to pick you up," he said decisively.

My tears had dried and I was nursing the baby when Peter came home. He rushed across the room to see his son.

"He looks just like me!" he shouted with joy.

"Of course he does, Peter, you *are* his father. Don't you see, this was meant to be? There was a purpose in our madness."

"You mean besides that fact that the sex was so good?" He grinned as he played with his son's long toes.

"Well, that too." I blushed. "But he was conceived in love, and I don't believe in accidents. Our chance meeting in the fertility clinic and the fact that the two of us brought this child into the world together was meant to be, just as we are meant to raise him *together*."

"Oh God, it's your spirit thing again, isn't it? Damn, Karen, I'm actually beginning to believe you. Did the spirit tell you what to name him?"

"It sure did—Peter Nicholas Latham, II."

LOST

Our son, John Rudolph Clemmons, Jr. looked just like his mother. He had her coal black hair and eyes. As soon as he started talking, the words came out in song. His grandfather said, "This boy was born to sing. Mark my words—he's gonna be a singer."

Johnny was barely out of diapers when Daddy taught him *The Bear Went Over the Mountain,* and every time he sang it, he danced around like a little clown, making everyone laugh. When they clapped, he puckered up and blew wet kisses.

We live on a mountain in North Carolina. When Johnny was almost three years old he was playing outside with his dog, Raleigh, when the two of them wandered off. The dog returned alone.

When I came home from work that day, I found my wife Melissa lying in the front yard by the swing, with Raleigh by her side. Mellie's legs were bleeding from scratches she got running through the woods. She told me she had called and screamed and cried. Now she was pale as a ghost, exhausted and barely able to whisper, "He's gone, Rudy. I can't find Johnny. I've looked everywhere. He was here with me one minute, and when I looked around he was gone."

I helped her up, took out my handkerchief, dried her tears and brushed the matted hair from her eyes. "Oh, he's just hiding from you, Mellie. You know how that little devil loves to hide. He's playing with you." I laughed. "Now stop crying and don't worry, I'll find him."

As a forest ranger, I knew this mountain like the back of my hand. I searched until it was too dark to see, and then I called my supervisor. Soon we had rangers and police officers scouring the area with rescue dogs, lights and bull horns. It had been below freezing each night, so after three days and nights, we knew there was no chance of finding our son alive.

***

Mingan and his cousins were on their way back home to the Cherokee reservation. They had been on a trip to the trading post near Black Mountain. Suddenly they heard a child cry and found a boy with raven hair and coal black eyes lying in a ravine where he had fallen.

Mingan jumped off his horse, scrambled down the cliff through the rhododendron and brought the child out. He tried to comfort the boy, to learn who he was and where he lived, but Mingan's efforts were useless. The boy was too frightened to talk and only screamed louder at the sight of Indians wearing war paint.

The sun was fast disappearing over the mountain and a cold wind whistled through the tall pines. There was no time to waste. Mingan held the shivering child close, wrapped him in his serape and set out for the reservation.

Luyu had cooked rabbit stew and baked a corn cake for supper. She and Mingan had recently lost their baby, and Luyu was inconsolable. He found her sitting by the fire, surrounded by the baskets she had been weaving, her feet tucked under her, tears in her eyes.

Mingan handed her the little boy. "He is a lost child. He is cold and hungry."

Luyu removed the boy's wet clothes and shoes, wrapped him in a blanket and fed him warm stew. She rocked him in her arms, and just before he fell asleep the child sang: *The bear went over the mountain to see what he could see. The other side of the mountain was all that he could see.*

Mingan told Luyu he wanted to take the child back to the trading post and make an effort to find his parents. A slight jerk of Luyu's shoulders showed her impatience with him. Her voice cracked when she said, "The spirits sent this child to *me*. His name will be Ysdi Yano—little bear."

***

After the third day of searching, I finally admitted that Johnny would not be found alive. I went home and collapsed, my head in Mellie's lap. Thankfully, I was married to a very strong woman. She stroked my hair. Neither of us spoke for a long time. Finally, she put her mouth soft against mine and said, "Rudy, this is too much for either of us to bear alone. We will get through it together."

My friends and I continued to search for my son's body. Johnny might have been attacked by wolves or wild dogs, but we never even found bones. Melissa and I kept hoping our little son found a way out of the forest, that maybe he was still alive somewhere. But eventually even that hope faded away.

Mellie created a memorial flower garden beside our house. She was a gifted gardener. She planted pinks, four-o'-clocks, verbena, heliotrope and others that I can't even name. I dug a fish pond and built a bench—a place where we found peace holding hands and remembering our lost son.

Kelli was born two years after we lost Johnny. She inherited my blond hair, so light it looked like duck fluff. She also inherited my fair skin, my freckles and my love of nature.

Kelli grew up knowing that she once had an older brother. She heard the story about how he was lost and felt the black cloud of grief hanging over our house. Mellie was determined that Johnny would never be forgotten. She kept the memorial garden full of beautiful flowers and every year she lit a candle on his birthday.

Our daughter was a tomboy. When she was old enough, I took her to work with me and taught her about life in the back country. I was responsible for overseeing a camp ground near Black Mountain, where we rangers watched for poachers, forest fires and anything unlawful.

Mellie learned to quilt—beautiful quilts, I might add. She sold them in gift shops nearby. They were big hits with the tourists who came looking for local crafts to carry home. But no matter how hard she tried, Mellie could not interest Kelli in needlework, not our daughter.

When school was out, Kelli took campground brochures around to stores and motels. She placed them in racks alongside brochures of *Unto These Hills, The Wax Museum, Ghost Town* and other attractions. She also worked at the Black Mountain campground collecting the small fee we charged campers to rent a space and buy firewood.

Mellie had four quilts that she wanted to place in a gift shop in Cherokee Village. The three of us took a break from our daily routine and drove up to the village for the weekend.

A statue of an Indian chief and a big stuffed black bear stood on either side of the shop door. The quilts were hung on a line strung across the back of the shop along with Indian blankets and other touristy souvenirs: children's Indian feather headdresses, toy drums, tomahawks, turquoise jewelry, beaded belts, moccasins trimmed with beads and hand-woven baskets.

After getting settled in our motel room, we went out for something to eat. We bought hot dogs at a little stand and ate them sitting on a bench overlooking the river.

The area offered attractions for tourists to learn firsthand about the Cherokee culture. Indian women were making pottery, painting gourds, weaving baskets and doing bead work. Not far from where we sat, we saw a bonfire and heard Indians chanting to the beat of drums.

Kelli left and went to investigate. She noticed that one of the young man looked different from his companions. She was intrigued and instinctively drawn to his side, where she found herself telling him the story of her long lost brother.

Just then someone yelled, "Come, Ysdi Yano, you are needed here!"

"I am sorry miss, I must go." The young man regarded her with open curiosity, then confided, "Your story interests me. I have always known that *I* had another family and have longed to meet my real mother and father. If you come to my house, maybe my father, Mingan, can answer your questions."

"See anything interesting?" Mellie asked when Kelli returned.

"Yes Mama, I sure did. I saw lots of Indians doing a stomp dance around a bonfire, but one of them was different. He didn't look like an Indian, although he wore war paint and his black hair was cut in a Mohawk with an eagle feather stuck in it. You won't believe what he told me, Mama. You have to come see him!"

Here we go again! I thought, *getting our hopes up, being let down and feeling the pain and grief all over again.*

In the twenty years since we lost Johnny, I had always tried to be realistic about our situation, so I said, "Kelli, it's not unusual for this young man to look different. After all, through the years the Cherokees often intermarried. At one time they even owned black slaves. They intermarried with them, and later with whites."

"But Daddy, I talked to him. He said he believed he had another family somewhere. He gave me his address and asked us to come talk to his father, Mingan."

Mellie's eyes grew big as saucers, her excitement growing by leaps and bounds.

"Let's go see him!" she cried.

"Okay, Mellie," I reluctantly agreed, "but don't rule out the possibility of this being another wild goose chase."

The stomp dance was over when we arrived at the bonfire. Everyone was quiet. The only sound was the crackle of flames flickering skyward. The tourists arranged themselves around the sacred fire and waited for the storyteller to begin. He spoke very clearly, so that all could hear his folk lore about a black bear.

When he finished, he motioned to a young man. "Come, Ysdi Yano, play your flute and sing the bear song."

The young man Kelli had described stepped forward. He lifted a cane flute with six holes and played a soft, mesmerizing melody.   Then he held the flute against his chest and began to sing: *The bear went over the mountain, the bear went over the mountain, the bear went over the mountain, to see what he could see, to see what he could see, to see what he could see. The other side of the mountain, the other side of the mountain, the other side of the mountain was all that he could see.*

Mellie gasped and grew limp at my side. She was plainly taken aback by the young man's song. I put my arm around her and held her close. I knew what she was thinking.   We watched as the crowd dispersed. The Indians laughed and talked among themselves, collected their things and left. We were alone.   None of us knew what to say or do.

That night in the motel Mellie said, "We have to talk to him, Rudy."

I agreed.

The following morning, we piled into my old Chevrolet. Kelli insisted on driving. I sat in front and Mellie was in back. I gripped the piece of paper with the address: Cabin #5 Lodge Road, Cherokee, North Carolina.

We found few road signs as we climbed into The Great Smokey Mountains.   I was nervous about meeting the young man, and Kelli's driving only made it worse. "Slow down Kelli! Can't you see that sign?" I yelled.

"Yes, Daddy. It says *Sharp Curve Ahead.*"

"There's another sign, Kellie. Slow down!"

"I see it, Daddy, and I can read: *Deer Crossing*. And there's another one that says, *Watch for Bears.*"

At last we came to a big green sign with white letters: *Cherokee Indian Reservation Five Miles Ahead.*

Five miles driving along winding mountain roads seemed like an eternity, but finally we stopped in front of cabin #5 on Lodge Road. A big yellow dog lay on the porch amid piles of white oak strips, hickory bark, honeysuckle vines and unfinished baskets.

"Well, here we are," our daughter announced.

Mellie and I were too frightened to move as we stared at the cabin door.

"Hey, don't worry. I'll go in and talk to him," Kelli offered. "Wish me luck!"

"Yeah," I murmured under my breath.

"God, I'm scared." Mellie confessed as she twisted her hands in her lap.

"Me too." Then I tried to calm my nerves with humor: "I just hope to hell he doesn't come out wearing a loin cloth."

We waited a long time before Kelli emerged from the cabin. She was smiling from ear to ear, carrying a baby. It was wrapped in a colorful blanket and strapped to a cradleboard. Under heavy black lashes, her little eyes gleamed like river rocks.

"Mama, Daddy, meet your granddaughter. Her name is Immokalee." Kelli beamed. "It means tumbling water."

Ysdi Yano followed, minus his eagle feather and war paint He was dressed in black pants, a red shirt and a serape. His arm was around a beautiful young woman with black braids that reached to her waist. She walked proudly by his side and smiled up at him as they approached our car. Behind them was a tall lanky Indian man.

Mellie and I climbed shakily out of the car to greet them.

The young man's lip quivered. "I may be atsutsa—lost atsutsa."

Mellie went to him and held his face between her hands. He smiled at her as she looked deep into his eyes, so like her own. She saw something that only a mother can see. Mellie kissed him gently on each cheek, and then she turned to me. Between sobs she said, "Rudy, we've found him! We've found Johnny!"

It was my turn then. The tears that I'd held inside me for so many years burst forth. My voice caught in my throat as I threw my arms around my son. All I could manage to say was, "Thank God."

JON AND JESSICA

Jessica was on the beach in front of her condo. She lay in a white plastic lounge chair, a book in one hand, a glass of Chardonnay in the other. She was listening to waves crash against the shore, watching the sun set far out over the Atlantic Ocean, and unwinding after a long day at *Jessica Harmon's Realty* on Sea Island Beach, South Carolina.

The sexy novel she was reading was set in Paris and featured a handsome, romantic Frenchman named Pierre Lefebvre. She was fantasizing an encounter with Pierre when she glanced down the beach, to where a man walking by the edge of the water was headed in her direction. Little waves splashed around his feet and soaked his rolled-up trouser legs as he came closer.

She pulled up the straps of her black swim suit and raised her hand to her forehead to block out the bright sun. With the dreamy image of Pierre still foremost in her mind, she shouted, "Hello!" over the waves crashing behind the stranger.

"Hello!" he called back, bringing her back to reality with his slow South Carolina drawl. "Pretty sunset, isn't it?"

"Sure is. Are you new to the area?"

"Yeah!" he yelled as a huge wave almost drowned out his voice. Several Plovers scattered around his bare feet as he strolled over and asked how her day had been.

"Pretty busy," she flirted. "And yours?"

"Not bad."

"Would you like some wine?" Luckily, Jessica always carried an extra glass in her beach bag.

He brushed the sand off his hands, sat in the chair beside her and took the glass she offered.

"I'm Jessica Harmon," she said.

"Good to meet you, I'm Jon Whitaker."

"Well, Jon, welcome to Sea Island."

He had strong broad shoulders and wore his light brown hair in a buzz cut. *Well, he's no Pierre,* she thought, *but he is cute, and being new to the area, maybe he'll be a new client.*

Jon Whitaker seemed tense and uneasy as his dark brown eyes darted from Jessica, to the sunset, and back again. He wrapped his long tapered fingers around the green-stemmed wine glass and brought it to his full sensuous lips, as though it were a thing to treasure, much the way Pierre Lefebvre might have sipped his Bordeaux in Paris.

The wine seemed to relax him as they watched the sun set together. Jessica tried to find out more about him, but he revealed very little, only that he grew up in a small coastal town nearby. When he asked about her, she told him she had lived in Sea Island all her life, was divorced with no children, and she owned a real estate company.

He asked if she had traveled a lot and what she liked to do for fun. They talked and watched the sunset color the water gold, pink and orange before dropping into the sea. She knew as she watched him walk away down the beach that he would be back.

And she was right. Eventually Jessica invited Jon in to see her condo, hoping to get to know him, perhaps tempt him with one of her listings?

He clearly liked not only Jessica, but also her shrimp cocktail, Brie, rosemary crackers, vodka tonics and music. She played *Dreaming of You* by Selena, which almost brought Jon to tears:

Late at night when all the world is sleeping, I stay up and think of you. And I wish on a star that somewhere you are thinking of me too.

Next he held her close and they danced to Whitney Houston singing:

I will always love you. I hope life treats you kind. And I hope you have all you dream of. And I wish you joy and happiness. But above all this, I wish you love

When she offered to drive him home, he refused, but agreed to meet her for breakfast the next morning at *The Balcony by the Bay.*

Jessica called her office to let them know she'd be out with a client.

At breakfast, Jon seemed to find joy in everything—watching the sea gulls fly around the boats in the bay, the Mimosas, Eggs Benedict, southern grits, hot biscuits, and especially her company.

She loved his boyish look, his laugh and the way his eyes sparkled when he looked at her. They lingered over second and third cups of coffee and celebrated their chance meeting on the beach.

Jon held her hand as they wandered aimlessly down the boardwalk, commenting on the weather, the traffic and the crowds. They visited gift shops, book stores and looked at seascapes in an art gallery. They ate chocolates from the Godiva store and ice cream on a bench outside Ben and Jerry's before he looked at his watch and said he had to run.

***

After they parted, Jon sneaked through the back door of *Davino's Deli.* He tied a clean apron around his waist, washed his hands and walked over to the preparation table, where he began chopping vegetables for the salad bar.

The waitress, Julie, a bit hung over from the night before, winked at Jon as she bent over the beverage counter, revealing her ample bosom. Larry, the druggie dishwasher, came in late as usual. And Leo, the owner, was in a nasty mood—probably because of his nagging wife. But, it was a job, and for the time being, Jon Whitaker was thankful to have it.

***

Jessica Harmon Realty was busy, and so was Jessica Harmon's mind. She wasn't thinking about selling houses, but about her new friend. She really liked Jon, but there was something mysterious about him.

Who was he anyway, and why did she care so much? Why couldn't she get him off her mind—a man she knew nothing about? For all she knew, he had a girlfriend, perhaps he was married, yet something drew her to him. And whatever it was, it would not let go.

She was on Jon's mind, too. He knew her office was on a side street in the busiest part of town. One day he walked by just to take a look. His heart pounded when he saw her car parked out front. He wanted more than anything in the world to walk in and see her beautiful face.

Jessica spent late afternoons on the beach trying to finish her book, but she had a hard time concentrating. She watched the passersby, hoping that the next one would be Jon.

His days at the deli were long and tiring. He came back to his room exhausted, but was unable to fall asleep. He sat by the window thinking:

At night when all the world is sleeping, I stay up and think of you. I wish upon a star that somewhere you are, thinking of me too

Jessica *was* thinking of him, and one night as she stood looking out her bay window at the stars twinkling in the sky over the ocean, she saw a man standing alone on the beach. He was staring her way. He stood there a long time before he slowly turned and walked away.

The next day she found several messages in her folder when she arrived at the office, one of them from her old boyfriend, Robert – *How about lunch at the Starfish at 12:30?*

She asked her secretary to call Robert and tell him she would be there. He had been asking her to marry him for years. It began with candlelight dinners, roses, whispered endearments, gifts of jewelry and cruises on his yacht. Now their relationship was like that of an old married couple. It left her feeling empty. He was a good man— kind and attentive—may too much so. Sometimes she wished he would just let her alone. But other times, when she was very lonely, she considered accepting his offer of marriage.

Robert was wealthy. He owned a marina, where he stored and serviced huge boats and yachts, including his own: *Robert's Rapture.* He had a beautiful home on a secluded point at the end of The Cloisters. He could give her anything she wanted, but Jessica didn't know what she wanted.

Robert was waiting at the restaurant when she arrived, wearing a loud floral shirt that he picked up on one of his trips to the islands. He wore a gold chain around his neck and a diamond ring on his little finger. His hair was getting thin and gray, and he had started combing it over to hide his baldness.

Jessica found him sitting at a table by the window. Robert always assumed he knew exactly what she wanted and what she needed, so he had already ordered a glass of Riesling for her.

She hated the way he decided things for her, and she hated the way he treated the waiter. Robert was arrogant and demanding, as though he wanted attention maybe.

She was gazing out the window, hardly listening to his endless chatter, when he said, "Jessie, I thought we might make a quick trip down to Bermuda over Labor Day Weekend, what do you think?"

A tall, broad-shouldered man with short brown hair was passing by outside. He looked like Jon. And then she was sure—it *was* Jon. The water she was drinking went down the wrong way and she started coughing.

"Jessie, are you okay?" Robert asked, but quickly dismissed his concern when she nodded. "Well, what do you think? We can leave on Thursday and come back Tuesday. It'll do you good. You need to get away."

She was still coughing from the water in her windpipe when she stupidly said, "Okay."

All the way back to the office, she kicked herself for agreeing to spend six days with Robert on his damn yacht. She must have been out of her mind.

When she walked in the door, one of her agents said, "Sounds like we're in for a big blow. Hurricane Ivan is headed this way, supposed to hit Wednesday night. We need to start boarding up the beachfront properties! "

At 5 PM Robert called: "Jessie, it looks like all bets are off for our trip. We're already making plans to button down the marina and move our boats to the hurricane hold. Sorry Babe, we'll reschedule soon."

Jessica couldn't decide if she was more upset about the pending hurricane, or relieved to have escaped the long weekend with Jon.

Either way, storm clouds rolled in early Wednesday afternoon. Jessica left work early and called the maintenance man to board up the windows in her condo. The wind was beginning to pick up and the sea was rough when she walked down to the beach to fetch her lounge chairs. By the time she had moved everything inside from her deck, the rain had begun. A weather man on TV was advising people to evacuate by 10 PM, before the bridge over the causeway closed.

Natives of Sea Island were used to this. Ivan wasn't predicted to be big enough to drive Jessica Harmon inland. She was always prepared. All she had to do was ride it out.

It was a perfect opportunity to finish her novel about romantic Pierre Lefebvre. But the more she read about him, the more arrogant and self-centered Pierre seemed. He was much like Robert, who required a younger woman like Jessica to show off like one of his possessions.

As the hurricane shook her condo and bent the palmetto trees from side to side, she thought again how grateful she was to Ivan for saving her from six boring days with Robert. If she didn't even want to spend six days with him, wasn't she an absolute idiot to consider spending the rest of her life with him?

When Jessica awoke the next morning, the sky was clear and the ocean calm. The town had already sent trucks to pick up the debris littering the beach, and the landscape people at her complex were removing limbs and trash from around the condos. The tourists, who had evacuated, would gradually reappear and life would return to normal in no time. She took her lounge chairs back down to the beach, where she would watch the sunset later.

She arrived at her office about 9AM, checked her calendar, and then remembered she had an appointment to show a house at The Cloisters at 1PM. *Davino's Deli* was on the way, so she decided to grab a salad before meeting her client. When she got to the salad counter, the bowl of mixed greens was empty and the line was at a standstill. Just then, Jon rushed out of the kitchen with some replacement salad.

Their eyes met at the same time. "Hi, Jess," he said bashfully.

"Jon! Hey, it's nice to see you. Did you survive the storm okay?"

"Yeah, old timers don't let a little storm like Ivan rattle us. Did you make out okay? Any damage?"

"Oh, nothing to speak of. I haven't seen you on the beach lately," she shyly added.

"Been busy," he said, glancing down at his apron.

Jessica quickly realized that Jon was ashamed of being caught out in his lowly job, and she desperately wanted to put him at ease. "Say, I just bought a great bottle of wine. Why don't we celebrate surviving the storm and open it on the beach after work?"

"Yeah, that'd be nice." He grinned.

The beach had been sweep clean. Jon walked up, kissed her cheek, and sat beside her like they'd never been apart. Even the sea oats looked refreshed. Beautiful shells that had been washed up from the dark ocean floor glistened in the sunlight. The tide crept silently toward them, leaving little puffs of white foam at their feet.

Later, Jessica led Jon inside where she encouraged him to undress her, caress her and make love to her. Afterwards, they lay side by side holding hands.

Jon feared they had no future together, considering the discrepancy in their social standing, but all he could think about was his hands caressing her luxurious hair and her soft skin against his.

The only sound he heard was her breathing, but then suddenly the flashbacks returned—the clanging metal doors slamming shut and locking, the cramped space, the horrible food, and the worst of all—the absence of a woman's love.

Jon could still see the clerk lying unconscious on the floor of the convenience store, the siren and the flashing blue lights of the police car, the cop yelling, "Drop your gun and put your hands over your head!"

He remembered his younger brother crying as the cops handcuffed him and threw him in the back of the squad car. He recalled the disgust in his parent's eyes during the trial and their visits to him in prison.

The tears rolling down the back of his neck were for all the people he had hurt, and for the years of happiness he had stupidly thrown away because of his drug and alcohol use.

He had taken advantage of every opportunity afforded him in prison and had managed to earn a degree, but he was still working in a lowly deli, living in one room, and was hopelessly in love with this woman lying beside him. He would not hurt her, too.

Jessica felt Jon's body grow tense. She heard his moan and sensed his anguish. She sat up cross- legged beside him, and in the remaining daylight, she saw how lovingly he looked at the body she had offered him.

Jon knew he had to tell her the truth, and when he had finished, absolute silence followed. He waited for what seemed like an eternity before Jessica gently took his face in her hands, kissed his eyelids, and rested her head on his chest. He felt her breath, her heartbeat, her tears, and her love. She rolled over, pulled him close, and held him in her arms, as though she had known all along.

CHARTREUSE BIKE

It was leaning against the steps leading to the apartment above the store. That apartment hadn't been rented in months, maybe even a year. It was a girl's bike, a yellowish green color with a rusty basket hanging over the dented front fender.

As a normal sixteen year old boy with a normal interest in girls, I had to check it out.

With the money I made mowing yards, I went into the store, bought a Dr. Pepper, a candy bar, and some bubble gum. I sat on the warehouse steps across the road where I had a good view of the apartment and watched for any movement. Soon a face appeared in the window. I waved, walked over and dropped two pieces of bubble gum into the bicycle basket.

The next day the bookmobile stopped in front of the store, so I rode my bike over to return a mystery. The girl was there. She had long blond hair pulled back in a ponytail tied with a pink ribbon. She asked the bookmobile lady for a library card.

"Are you new here?" the lady asked.

"Yes, ma'am."

"Name?"

"Rose Ellerby."

Rose checked out two books and hurried to the door. Her sad blue eyes met mine as she passed, and I was pretty sure she recognized me as the creep who spied on her from the warehouse steps.

The next day I had to mow old lady Miller's yard, which took most of the day. Then I had to trim her hedge and carry the clippings down to a gully below her house. It was really late when I finished. After supper, I decided to do a little snooping in the dark and discovered an old Chevrolet parked beside the girl's bike.

Through the apartment window, I saw a light bulb hanging over a table where Rose and a woman were eating. Next the sheriff's car drove up. He walked up the stairs, knocked and went in. Wow, way cool!

Later that week, I left a box of Crackerjacks and a note in her bicycle basket: *Rose, my name is Tim. Will you go riding with me? I'll be here tomorrow at 3:00.*

I rode my bike over and waited on the warehouse steps forever, thinking I'd been stood up. But before long she came down, got her bike and walked across the road.

"Want to ride to the park?" I asked.

"Yeah, I guess," she said.

I did most of the talking, while she said almost nothing.

Finally I asked, "Want to go back to the store for some ice cream?"

"Yeah, I guess," she said.

When we returned to her apartment, the sheriff's car was there again. I decided not to mention it, but my curiosity was killing me.

We went into the store, where I bought two Dixie Cups from the ice cream box and took two wooden spoons from the jar on top. We went outside and sat on a bench not far from the air pump and a pile of empty motor oil cans. Soon a beautiful woman, who walked with a limp, came around the corner and said, "Rose, honey, it's okay to come back now."

I forgot about Rose for a while because Mama, Daddy, my sister and I went to the beach for a week. When we returned it was time for school to start. The first day of school was bright and sunny, and I was excited about beginning a brand new year. The only seats left on the bus were at the very back. When it stopped at Rose's corner, she walked back and sat right beside me. "Hi Rose." I said.

"Hi Tim," she answered with a shy smile.

She wore a white blouse, a yellow shirt, and a matching ribbon in her hair. She was the prettiest girl I had ever seen. She had on pale pink lipstick and something that smelled nice and sweet. But her sad look was still there, so I figured she was dreading her first day in a new school.

It turned out we were both in Mrs. Jones' tenth grade class, so we sat together in the back of the room. The cliquish girls just stared at Rose and made no effort to be friendly. At lunchtime, I showed her the way to the cafeteria and sat with her.

Our class bully was a boy named Roger. He loved to taunt girls and anybody smaller than he was. I saw him watching Rose and suspected he was preparing to launch some spitballs in her direction. If he dared, he'd have to deal with me and I was big enough to knock his block off.

It was the second week of school. Rose and I were at our lockers getting out books for our two o'clock class when the attack finally happened. Only it wasn't initiated by Roger. Instead, nasty little Millie shoved Rose, slamming her face against the metal door, cutting her lip and making her nose bleed.

I got some paper towels from the boy's bathroom, held them against Rose's nose and led her to the principal's office.

Mrs. Douglas, the secretary, put pressure on her nose until the bleeding stopped. The principal called Millie to the office and made her apologize. I took the opportunity to give Millie a mean look, sending a message that I wasn't above beating up on a girl. Rose's blouse was splattered with blood, and she was pale as a ghost when the three o'clock bell rang. I put my arm around her and said, "Let's go home, Rose."

When we got to Rose's apartment, her mother was away at work. I knew my mom, who had a heart of gold, would take good care of her. Mama got Rose cleaned up and into a robe while she put her clothes in the washing machine. I fixed snacks, took Rose to the den and tried to calm her down.

The snotty girls at school remained unfriendly, but nobody bothered Rose again. They knew they'd have me to deal with if they misbehaved. In the meantime, Rose started coming home with me after school, so we could do homework together.

As the weeks went by, Rose Ellerby remained a mystery. I did learn her favorite color was pink, her favorite food was French fries and she loved to read as much as I did. Eventually she relaxed enough to laugh and giggle at my corny jokes

I continued to leave notes and treats in her bicycle basket. We rode to the park on warm afternoons. That's where I got my first kiss and where she finally told me her secret.

"We moved here to hide from my daddy," she confessed. "He beat my mama and shot her in the leg. When he was arrested, he said if she allowed him go to prison, he'd kill her when he got out. Well, now he's been released. Mama took out a restraining order, and Sheriff Boyd is trying to keep us safe."

The Monday before Thanksgiving, Rose did not get on the bus. I worried all day thinking she might be sick, alone, cold and hungry. Snow was falling, landing on my coat and cap as I climbed the steps to her apartment.

When I knocked, the door opened slowly. A man's hand grabbed me and pulled me in. His other hand held a gun pointed at my face.

He wore dirty jeans, a plaid shirt and had greasy hair with Conway Twitty sideburns.

"Well, what do we have here? Is this your little friend, Rosie?"

I was too shocked to understand what was happening until I saw Angie, Rose's mom, and Rose tied to chairs. They had rags stuffed in their mouths. I saw terror in Rose's eyes. Angie's clothes were torn and her head was slumped down over her chest. One of Angie's eyes was swollen shut and there were bruises all over her arms and legs.

I'm going to die, I thought as Clarence Ellerby shoved me down into a chair. He had been sitting on the sofa, drinking liquor straight from the bottle and was so drunk he could barely stand. When he tied me up, my coat padded my arms, leaving the ropes so loose I knew I could escape. He shoved a dishrag in my mouth, turned the oil stove up high and then passed out on the sofa.

I glanced around at the mess. Dirty dishes covered the table. Some still held food scraps and Clarence's cigarette butts. The venetian blinds were askew, a broken lamp lay on the floor next to Rose's school books and the pages from her notebook were scattered all over the floor.

When Clarence started to snore, I squirmed free of the ropes, pulled the rag from my mouth, tiptoed to the sofa, snatched the gun and ran out the door. The snow was really coming down hard by then, so I almost fell as I rushed down the steps to the store. I asked the owner to call the sheriff, who arrived in fifteen minutes with three deputies. I handed them Clarence's gun, then sneaked up the stairs behind them to see what would happen.

By the time the police entered the apartment, Clarence was holding a knife to Angie's throat. Sheriff Boyd yelled, "Drop the knife Clarence!"

Clarence was eyeing the gun pointed at him, trying to figure out his next move, so he didn't notice when one of the officers slowly picked up the liquor bottle. The officer eased behind him, grabbed his arm, raised the bottle and came down hard on his head.

Somehow Clarence staggered loose and bolted toward the door. Only then did Sheriff Boyd fire the shot that entered Clarence's left temple, opening up a big hole in his head. Blood spattered across the wall and left ruby colored puddles on the floor.

I barely made it to the bathroom before I threw up.

One of the deputies radioed for an ambulance for Clarence. Sheriff Boyd took Angie and Rose to the hospital, where Angie was treated for a broken arm and cuts and bruises.

The next day Mama called the principal and asked him to excuse Rose and me until the week after Thanksgiving.

Much to my surprise, the town newspaper sent a reporter to interview me. They wanted to hear my side of the story, which ran with my picture and a caption: *LOCAL BOY SHOWS BRAVERY IN HOSTAGE SITUATION.*

Brave boy my ass! I was a damn basket case. My nerves were shot to hell. I cried all day and most of the next, with Mama's arms around me as she patted me on the back. I couldn't sleep or stop thinking how close I came to being killed. It was the first time I had seen an actual dead man, much less one with his head blown away.

I didn't want Rose to see what a baby I turned out to be, but Mama just wouldn't rest until she talked Angie and Rose into coming to our house for Thanksgiving dinner.

Angie was still a nervous wreck, and she tried hard not to cry. Her arm was in a cast, the bruises on her face and body had begun to fade, but I knew the horror was forever etched in her memory—in mine and Rose's too, for that matter.

Mama and Daddy were kind and respectful, but none of us knew what to say or how to act. It was the first time in my life that I didn't feel like eating Thanksgiving dinner.

I longed to escape to the park, feel the cold November wind whip against my face and blow through my hair, be a normal sixteen year old boy again. At that moment, I glanced across the table at Rose. She had a calm brave look on her face. She winked at me. I knew the chartreuse bike was parked out front beside mine. I asked Mama if we could be excused.

LIVING IN TECHNICOLOR

Marci pulled into the student parking lot at 8:15, zipped her parker and pulled the hood over her head before stepping out into the cold wind blowing around the Arts building. Students were rushing to make their 8:30 classes. The bell rang just as she entered room 215 and placed her assignment on the table in front of Dr. Michael Cooper's desk. On her design board were swatches of fabric: solid rust for the two sofas and a paisley for the three chairs. The carpet sample was the same shade of blue in the paisley and there were photos of the paintings she planned for the bank lobby.

Michael winked at her and whispered, "See you at the deli." Most Tuesdays and Thursdays they met for lunch, and that day was no exception. But this time when they finished eating he said, "Hey, Marci, meet me at my apartment at 5:00. It won't hurt if you get home late one time."

"I can't, Michael. I have a husband and two children. Our lunches together are as far as I can go. I love my husband. I'm sorry."

***

The bottom half of the smashed bottle rolled over shards of green glass and red wine that had splashed across the tile floor. The top of the bottle and the cork shot across the room and hit the wall. "God damn it!" Andy yelled. "Are you trying to kill me?"

Marci Kennedy's husband had just admitted to having an affair. She had been in denial, telling herself he would never betray her, ignoring little clues until she found the tube of hot pink lipstick under their bed. Then she remembered his locked metal box in the basement and searched until she found the key.

Inside were a notebook of love poems in Andy's handwriting and a photo of a woman with bleached hair and hot pink lipstick. Beneath the notebook she found a little plastic bag filled with white powder.

Marci had those discoveries spread out on the kitchen table when Andy came home from work. At first he was too stunned to talk, but then he confessed. The other woman's name was Crystal, a co-worker. They had the audacity to meet at Marci and Andy's home on their lunch break, where they had sex and used cocaine.

"Leave!" she screamed. "Get out of my sight!" As he turned to go, she threw the bottle. Her heart was as shattered as the glass that lay on her kitchen floor.

***

Marci and Andy had been high school sweethearts. They had planned their future together: she would work and help pay his way through college, and once he had a degree and a good job, he would help her achieve her dream of becoming an interior designer.

They moved into student housing. Andy, a bright guy, made good grades and excelled in all his classes. He found a part time job on campus, while Marci took a job in a manufacturing company as secretary to an obnoxious man who thought women belonged at home— barefoot and pregnant.

When Andy was a junior, Marci did get pregnant. She delayed telling her boss as long as she could, but when she started showing, he fired her.

The college gave her a temporary job in a typing pool, while Andy worked as an assistant to his chemistry professor in addition to the part time job he already had.

Their little girl was born premature, and things were touch and go with the baby and the bills. Marci spent many harried days and sleepless nights before the child was finally healthy.

In her spare time, what little there was, she typed Andy's papers and sometimes those of his classmates.

Before the end of his senior year, Marci was pregnant again with another little girl. Andy got his degree and a good job. As the years went by, her life revolved around her children and her husband, who seemed to have forgotten about her dream.

Both girls were in high school when Marci enrolled in a community college taking the basic classes required to enter a college that offered an interior design course.

After she learned of Andy's affair, she was so angry and depressed she could hardly function, but with weekly visits to a therapist and medication, she managed to complete the last few hours she needed to graduate.

The divorce was easy. Marci got the house, a nice settlement and the courage to start living *her* life—no longer in the dull gray of Andy's shadow, but in *Technicolor.*

She got a new hair style that gave her a youthful, natural look. She bought new clothes in colors that accented her lavender eyes and revealed the curvy body that she had kept hidden. She bought a red convertible to drive to her new job at Barnaby Interiors, LLC.

Robert Barnaby picked Marci to decorate a new house on Lake Norman. He gave her a copy of the floor plan to study and made an appointment for her to meet the owner, Leo Thornton.

The sky was dark and threatening when Marci found the turnoff to Leo Thornton's house. She followed the driveway through a wooded area and up to a large, two-story modern structure with glass that allowed one to see right through the house to the lake. She used her key and the security code to let herself in and wait for the owner.

From the great room, she watched the wind blow trees back and forth, whip the lake into a frenzy and send waves rolling up the beach.

Rain was coming down in sheets and a clap of thunder shook the house when a man swept through the front door, letting in a gust of wind that blew through the foyer. He wore a thin, rain- soaked blue shirt that clung to his chest. His dark hair was pulled back into a pony tail. "Mrs. Kennedy, I am Linwood Thornton," he said.

"Oh, they told me your name was Leo."

"Leo is my brother. He's away now. I am the architect and his stand-in, so to speak, so I'll be working with you until he returns." Linwood dried his hands and face on paper towels.

"Leo has pretty much left everything up to me, so let me tell you what I envision for the house. Let's start with the great room. It will be painted antique white. Auvergne, ochre and sage should be on your color pallet, with some variation of those colors used to create a harmonious flow throughout the house. For instance, the master bedroom should be done in sage and coral, accented with a soft, creamy white.

"Leo has an extensive collection of modern art, so I have designed the house with the paintings in mind. Many will be displayed in the long entrance hall, but we'll get to that later. My brother has also collected five or six pieces of Dale Chihully glass, which will be displayed on pedestals in and around the lower level."

Linwood also explained that the huge expanses of glass were designed to let in natural light, enhance the uniqueness of the space, and to provide a magnificent view of the lake.

Marci watched his long, slender, artistic fingers sweep in one direction and then another as he described his work. His intense green eyes lit up with excitement at the lighted stained glass window in the stairwell, which was reminiscence of the work of Frank Lloyd Wright.

By then it had stopped raining and sun was popping through the trees, shining across the rain soaked deck. "Oh, by the way," Linwood said, "we'll need some handsome deck furniture. Put that on your *to do* list. Choose something with soft, comfortable cushions to sit in to sip wine and watch the sun set over Lake Norman."

Linwood's light blue shirt was drying against his tan chest, and Marci noticed a faint, musky, masculine scent that made her hand shake as she wrote *deck furniture* on her note pad and told herself to *get a grip.*

"Well, I guess we've made a pretty good start. Why don't we meet here one week from today and see where we stand? Bring all your swatches, samples and photos." He handed her a card: *LINWOOD A. THORNTON, Architect.* "Please call if you have any questions."

Marci had assembled upholstery, carpet, paint samples, and photos of a perfect set of teak furniture for Leo's covered deck by the time she went back to meet Linwood Thornton.

When she arrived in his driveway, she saw two men sitting in a car with a government license tag. They wore black uniforms, and when they stepped from the car, she realized each man had a gun strapped to his waist.

The taller one pulled off his sun glasses, flashed a badge and said, "FBI. We need to search your car and ask you some questions about Leo Thornton. Do you know where he is?"

"No, I don't even know him," Marci replied.

"Then what's your business here?"

"I'm employed by Barnaby Designs. I've been hired to decorate the house," she said, feeling intimidated.

"Do you know Linwood Thornton?"

"Yes."

The heavy-set man mumbled something and said, "What's your relationship to him?"

"Look, I'm only here to decorate this house. I don't have a relationship with either of the Thorntons."

Just then Linwood drove up and gave her a nervous smile. The two men demanded to see the house, so he opened the door and let them in. He motioned that she should enter, too, but Marci lingered in the hall as the three men did a thorough inspection.

Linwood looked pale and upset when they finally left.

"What is going on?" Marci demanded.

But he brushed her off. "Oh, it's nothing to worry about. Why don't you show me what you brought?"

Linwood's hands shook as he flipped through the samples, finally pulling out the ones he liked. Marci was still uneasy, but she took out her calculator to estimate prices.

"Okay, let's have the carpet installed and order the furniture made. I like the deck furniture, so go ahead and have it delivered. Call and give me a time line on all of it."

He pushed a lock of hair off his forehead and calmed down enough to manage a little smile. "I really like what you've done, Marci. I can see we're on the same page. Please call me Lin."

Later that week, she called Lin to tell him when the carpet would be installed and that the deck furniture would be delivered that afternoon.

"I have a lot on my plate now, Marci, but I do need to meet with you to get an up-date. Also, I really want to see that deck furniture. Can you meet me at the house at 5:00?" When she answered *yes*, he said, more or less to himself, "Okay, that'll be good."

That afternoon Lin looked every bit the artist in a gray silk suit with a colorful scarf around his neck. He brought out a bottle of wine and two glasses with long thin amber stems. They went to the deck, where they sat in new chairs with floral cushions, under the shade of a turquoise umbrella. He sipped the chilled wine and seemed to relax a little.

"Why is the FBI looking for Leo? Do you know when your brother's coming back?" Marci could not keep herself from asking.

"Yes—well, no. Not really," he stuttered.

Marci wondered why Lin was being so secretive, why he didn't seem concerned about whether or not Leo would like what they were doing to his house, or how they were spending his money. What if Leo was dead? Maybe Linwood Thornton wasn't who he said he was? Maybe she should be very afraid of him!

Part of the carpet had been installed and the rest was being delivered piecemeal. Next they were expecting furnishings for four bedrooms, a game room, an office, a library, the great room and a large dining room that overlooked the lake on the north side of the house.

One afternoon, Marci had come to the house to meet a delivery truck bringing the dining room furniture, when Lin suddenly appeared. He began watching the men remove a quilted cover from the table, and then his phone rang.

"Lin Thornton here," she heard him answer. "You've cleared it? Then I can come get it? The key is at the marina? Yes, thank you."

After the truck pulled away, Lin said, "Marci, I need a really big favor. Can you to drive me over to J.D.'s Marina? I have to pick up my new boat. I saved up for years to buy this Boston Whaler, had to design a lot of rich folk's houses to earn the cash. I only bought it now because my brother has a dock where I can actually moor it. Can't wait to show you, Marci. I'll bring it home by water, but will you please wait at the house until I get back? I have something very important to discuss with you...

"Oh, by the way," he added, "I know of a great seafood restaurant near the marina. I'll bring something home for our supper. Open the bottle of wine in the fridge and enjoy a glass while you wait."

Marci took her wine to the deck and waited for Lin. It was beginning to get dark. The lake was busy with boaters coming in after a day of fun or fishing. Some were headed to a lakeside restaurant for drinks and dinner.

As she watched dark shadows fall across the water, Marci felt uneasy and anxious. She wasn't just curious anymore, she was fearful and needed to know what was going on with Lin and his brother.

When Lin finally arrived and had tied his shiny new boat at the dock, he took two Styrofoam trays from a bag and placed them on the new table. They ate in awkward silence until she said, "Lin, tell me what's going on, or I'm outta here."

"I'm so sorry, Marci..." Lin took a deep breath. "There's no easy way to say this, so I'll just lay it out. Leo has been smuggling drugs from the Mexican border to Lake Norman, and ICE has just arrested him in Arizona.

"At first the FBI suspected me, my parents and even you of being involved. My attorney and I are leaving for Phoenix tomorrow to attend his trial. They have no proof whatsoever that I was involved, because I wasn't, but the agents will try to prove this house was purchased with drug money. They will try to include it in asset forfeiture. But I feel like this house is *my baby*. If they take it away, it will break my heart.

"So I need your support, Marci. Trust me, please. Stay here and help finish the hard work we've started together. Take care of things until I return. You can sit on the deck, watch the sunset, and think positive thoughts that when I come home, we'll have something to celebrate."

Marci agreed to stay at the house while Lin attended the trial. She managed to keep busy, but she missed Lin so much. As the days turned into two weeks, she realized how much they completed each other, even read each other's minds.

Finally, the master bedroom furniture was delivered. It was more beautiful than she had envisioned when the delivery men placed it on the sage carpet. Marci made the bed with coral sheets and a coral, turquoise and sage bedspread complimented by a creamy, silk throw across the foot.

She sat in a chair covered in an ivory upholstery embroidered with seashells scalloped with a hint of coral, and thought about Lin. At the same time, she told herself that after all the heartache she's endured with Andy—the unfaithfulness and the divorce—how foolish was she to again trust her heart to a man?

Tears filled her eyes as watched a boat sail across the lake. Too soon Lin would sign the Barnaby Designs forms approving her work, and then what?

At that moment, her phone rang.

"Marci, I just landed at Charlotte airport. Are you all right? I missed you so much. Is everything okay there?"

"The house is all done. I just finished the master bedroom. It's beautiful, Lin. Can't wait to show it to you!"

"Don't move. I'll be there in 40 minutes."

It seemed like an eternity before he came rushing in and yelled, "Marci, I'm back!"

He looked like a different man. He was tired, but smiling, and the stress lines were gone. He wore jeans, a wide leather belt with a silver buckle, and flip flops.

Lin kissed her, popped the cork from a bottle of champagne, got two glasses and led her to the deck. "I know I've been gone a long time, but I had a lot to do, and I have so much to tell you...

"When Leo signed the papers at the closing on this house, he put down a twenty percent deposit, signed the mortgage papers, walked out of the attorney's office, and then completely disappeared. That's nothing new for Leo Thornton. My brother has pulled stuff like that all his life, always been in trouble, but managed to bounce back, with Mom and Dad's help—and mine. But this time he went too far.

"The FBI was already on Leo's tail at the closing. So they know he never lived in this house. The prosecutors could not prove it was ever used for any criminal activity. Long story short—the bank let me assume Leo's loan. The house is mine now!"

"That's wonderful, Lin, but how is that possible? I was sure the government would confiscate it."

He shook his head and stared into his glass of champagne. "I got lucky, Marci, but it cost me. As one agent put it, the FBI is not in the real estate business and has no interest in repossessing a house that's only twenty percent paid for. The bank, on the other hand, wanted the sale and allowed me to assume the mortgage with the same terms they offered Leo. I needed to qualify financially for the monthly payments—which I did—and then come up with the twenty percent. So I'm afraid I had to sell my Boston Whaler, Marci."

"But you loved that boat, Lin. Are you okay with this?"

He lifted his head, grinning ear to ear. "You kidding me? What good's a boat without a dock? Besides, you and I made this house together, right? My architectural design, your interior decoration. No boat comes close to that."

Marci mumbled in agreement as she struggled to keep her emotions in check.

"The Feds took Leo's old house. Everything he owned went into asset forfeiture, including his art collection. So I guess we'll have to find some other way to fill the long hallway. Maybe you could help me with that, Marci."

They held hands and sat quietly watching the sun slowly sink behind Lake Norman. Finally, Lin kissed her and said, "Marci, I want to see the bedroom."

They went inside, locked the door behind them, walked up the circular stairs and passed the stained glass window that cast a kaleidoscope of colors on their path to the future.

DOUBLE TROUBLE

Running, escaping, hiding—call it what you will—I was getting as far away as possible from my obsessive, controlling ex-husband, Marshall. So I was on my way to find the little cabin I had arranged to rent in the mountains of North Carolina.

My first twenty five years of life had been spent in sunny Florida. I had never even been near a mountain, and now I was driving on steep, icy, winding hair pin curves. As I climbed higher into the low lying clouds, my ears popped.

A mixture of sleet and snow made the road slick and treacherous. The car windows were fogged and I could barely see through the icy mess the windshield wipers pushed back and forth. Making matters even worse, the swaying U-Haul behind my car made the car jerk this way and that.

I was in real danger of getting too close to the edge and sliding down the mountain into the wilderness below.

My hands shook as I tried to steady my car and keep it on the icy road.

Desperate for a place to stop, I was elated to see a sign: *Bascom's Quick Stop: Rest Rooms, Gas, Eats, Apples and Cider.* I pulled off the road into one of the parking spaces and stepped into to a wintery blast that blew up my jeans and watered my eyes. This was the first time I had ever seen snow. I raised my face to the pale gray sky, opened my mouth and stuck my tongue out in wonder.

Country and western music, the sweet smell of something baking and hot coffee greeted me when I entered the warm little café.

After making a mad dash for the restroom, I slid into a booth, pulled my sweater close around me and waited for a waitress

"My Lord, where's your coat honey? What can I get you?" asked a frumpy middle aged woman with salt and pepper hair.

"I don't have a coat, and you can get me a cup of the hottest coffee you have, please."

"Got some good pecan pie," she said. "Just took it out of the oven."

"Okay, never had any pecan pie, but I'll give it a try. By the way, how far am I from Reynolds Ridge Road?"

"You done passed it, sweetie. Turn around and go back about a mile. It's a long winding dirt road. Only thing up there is the farm house and an itty bitty cabin they rent out."

My nerves were shot to hell by the time I finally found the cabin. Then I continued up the mountain to the Reynolds residence to get the key. I pulled my sweater tight against the mountain chill and knocked on the door, half expecting some hillbilly pervert to greet me.

Instead it was opened by a handsome young man with thick black hair and a face like a Roman god. His green eyes smiled as he rubbed his finger down the bridge of a nose that looked like it had been chiseled from Italian marble.

"I'm Liana Miller," I told him, "and I'm here to get the key to the cabin."

"Well, hello, Miss Miller, it's nice to meet you. Sorry you had to drive in this horrible weather. I'll go down and open up for you. The steps will be icy and it'll be freezing inside. I'll build a fire and help you get your things in."

I stared while he pulled on a navy blue pea jacket and a cap with fur lined flaps that covered his ears and the dark curly hair that brushed the top of his collar.

"I'll ride down with you, then walk back up," he continued. "I need the exercise, been on the computer all day."

The cabin was cold all right, but my handsome landlord soon had a roaring fire going in the big stone fireplace.

"We always stock the kitchen with a few things like milk, eggs, bread and coffee," he said. "I'll go make coffee and throw in a splash of bourbon to warm you up. Take off your shoes and toast your toes. I'll be right back."

We never had a fireplace in Florida. I got as close as I could and put my feet on the raised hearth. Soon it was so warm the rivets in my blue jeans were hot and my wool sweater smelled singed.

From the kitchenette, he asked softly, "Are you getting warm?"

When he returned, he rubbed his finger down the narrow bridge of his nose and handed me a mug. "What brings you Reynolds Ridge, Liana?"

I hesitated only a moment, then decided to confide in him. "I just went through a nasty divorce and I'm starting over. I've always wanted to be a potter. The Penland School for Crafts popped up when I was surfing the internet. I signed up to take a class, and here I am."

"Want to be a potter, huh? Well, you've come to the right place. We're only five miles from the campus. I'll show you how to go the back way."

A scratching noise at the front door made me jump. "Oh, lord, do you have bears up here?"

He chuckled, "Yeah, we do sometimes, but that isn't one of them. Bears are much bolder. Besides, they're hibernating now. That'll be my dog, Oggy."

Oggy proved to be a small black and brown terrier with wet hair and muddy feet. He walked in and jumped on the sofa like it belonged to him.

The fire felt good as it crackled in the hearth and sent sparks flying up the chimney. We sipped bourbon-laced coffee and shelled roasted peanuts from a bowl on the table between us, threw the shells in the fire, watched them burn and laughed like two old friends.

As he was leaving, he gave me a crooked grin, put a hand on my shoulder. "I'm glad you're here, Liana. I hope you'll like it."

"Me too! I want to know more about this place. Can you come down tomorrow evening for a glass of wine and tell me more?"

I spent the next day unloading the U-Haul and getting used to my new home. The nearest food store was only a mile away. I bought a bottle of wine, some cheese and crackers, and doggie treats for Oggy.

At exactly 5:00 my landlord knocked on the door. He pulled off his muddy shoes and tiptoed through the room in his stocking feet. Oggy followed. His little toenails clicked across the floor to the sofa.

I opened the Cabernet Sauvignon and poured two glasses, then we settled in front of a roaring fire with our feet propped on the hearth.

"This is great wine," he said as he rubbed his foot against mine, making me tingle all over.

The next morning I noticed the snow had picked up during the night and now covered the ground with several inches. I was making a pot of coffee and heating an English muffin when I heard a knock at the door. My Roman God landlord walked in, poured himself a cup and sat at the table beside me.

"I'll drive you to Penland today in my four-wheeler," he offered.

"Won't classes be canceled?"

"Liana, here in the mountains we don't cancel things just because of a little snow. Besides, it'll probably stop by noon. Get dressed and let's go."

But it was still snowing and the sky had darkened to nearly black when he drove me home that afternoon. I invited him in, put a pizza in the oven, poured two glasses of wine and warmed myself by the fire.

Outside eight inches of snow lay on the ground. Tree limbs and power lines were bent under a heavy white blanket.

The room smelled faintly of wood smoke. I was listening to embers crackling on the hearth and resting my head on the back of my chair, in a state of heavenly bliss, when suddenly the lights flickered and the room went dark.

We lit an oil lamp, stole a quilt from the bedroom, moved to the sofa and wrapped the quilt around our shoulders. He pulled me close. I felt his warm breath on my face and his lips brushed mine. Then suddenly someone knocked on the door.

He tensed, grunted and went to the door. In a low muffled voice, he asked, "What the hell are *you* doing here?"

"The power is out, man. I'm not staying in that dark cold house by myself."

The man standing in the doorway was well over six feet tall, with shoulders hunched against the mountain chill and Oggy nestled in his arms. He had the same chiseled profile and green eyes as the man sitting next to me. His long handsome nose was reddened from the cold and his black hair curled around his face and down his neck.

The newcomer hummed as he pulled off his navy blue pea jacket and cap with fur flaps. He draped them on a hook beside the door, where the other navy jacket and cap with fur flaps already hung.

Next he greeted me with supreme confidence and gently patted my hand. "I'm Tristan, your landlord," he said. "Welcome to Reynolds Ridge."

I looked at the man beside me on the couch and asked, "So who the hell are you?"

The man who had just kissed me shrugged, rubbed his finger down the bridge of his nose and with an amused look, said, "I'm Tracy."

"What's going on? Are you guys twins?"

Tracy put another log on the fire, sat back down beside me and pulled the quilt back around our shoulders.

"Do you have any more wine?" asked Tristan.

"Yes," I said. "And there's more pizza, but it's cold."

Tristan got a glass of wine, a slice of pizza and came to sit on the other side of me. "This is cozy," he said as he pulled the other end of the quilt around him, snuggled up and started humming again.

"Well," Tracy said, "don't get too cozy, buddy, because you're not staying."

"Says who, asshole? Good pizza, Liana," Tristan commented, ignoring his look-alike.

The men took turns telling mountain tales. We drank wine and laughed until well after midnight. It was still snowing like crazy and obviously nobody was going anywhere anytime soon. Besides, both men had drunk way too much wine to venture out into the weather.

I gathered up all the quilts I could find and made a cozy nest in front of the hearth. I remember lying down and pulling the quilts around me, but not much else until sometime during the night the man on my left stirred. I felt his wine breath on my face, then I stretched, arched my back and turned over. The one on the other side murmured something in his sleep and breathed pepperoni and onions on me.

Much later, I felt a chilly draft when one of them lifted the quilts and got up to throw logs on the fire. I wasn't quite conscious when he crawled back under the quilts. I did feel a cold hand slide down my backside and a hairy leg tickle my thigh. Oggy snuggled at my feet like a hot brick. Somebody did a lot of scratching, and I don't think it was the dog.

It was still snowing when I woke to the smell of coffee and bacon coming from the charcoal grill on the back porch. One of my landlords was boiling coffee and frying bacon. The other one was still snuggled against my back keeping me warm.

We had just finished eating breakfast on the coffee table we had pulled in front of the fireplace when someone said, "Go feed the horses."

"I fed them last night, asshole. You go."

This argument continued until one of them got up, put on his navy coat and cap with fur lined ear flaps and stomped out, slamming the door so hard the whole cabin shook.

In no time, he was back, brushing off the snow that had fallen on his coat. "We got ourselves a real blizzard. I predicted this was going to happen and so did the wooly worms."

"Nobody asked you for your meteorological prediction, you bloody simpleton."

"What's a wooly worm?" I asked, but got no answer.

"It's flooded," the first twin said.

"What's flooded?" his brother asked.

"The whole downstairs up at the house. The pipes under the kitchen sink burst."

"Holy crap," the other one said. They both pulled on their coats and caps and ran up the mountain to the big house.

It was still snowing in the late afternoon when they returned with boxes of food from their refrigerator, canned goods, a bag of dog food and enough beer and wine to sweeten the long days that lay ahead. They also brought a transistor radio, a box of cassettes, a Scrabble game and a Monopoly set.

"There's about an inch of water all over the downstairs. We did get the water turned off, but it'll be days before we have power again and even longer before a plumber can get up the mountain," one grunted. "Well, what the hell, we might as well party!"

Tristan—at least, I think it was Tristan—placed a pack of frozen hamburger meat by the fire next to the snow I was thawing for drinking water. The other one brought in an armload of wood, leaving me to sit and wonder what the bloody hell I had gotten myself into.

One of the guys put a cassette in the player and Van Morrison sang *Brown Eyed Girl.* Then they played *Killing Me Softly with His Song.* I was feeling seriously claustrophobic and wondering whether I could get away with killing them both, but then I would probably starve or freeze to death up here in the North Carolina backwoods all by myself.

We listened to *The Best of My Love* while eating hamburgers and drinking Coor's Lite laced with ice crystals.

All the beer sent us to the bathroom a lot, until the toilet stopped flushing.

The twin's bodies were so attuned that their bladders needed empting in unison. They raced to the front porch, aimed for the mouth of the pink pig yard art, and then raced back inside breathing icy white breath, zipping their pants and arguing about which one was the best shot.

I, on the other hand, went to the freezing cold bathroom to squat over a blue plastic bucket, while shivering so hard my teeth rattled. Oggy marked his spot beneath a boxwood tree, where he had turned the snow a brilliant shade of yellow.

We played Monopoly for hours. Tristan hummed as he got rich buying hotels and other properties. Tracy screwed up his face and groaned as he and I managed to pass *go*, collect two hundred dollars and some *get out of jail free* cards.

We drank wine and ate peanuts until I didn't give a rat's fuzzy ass about anything anymore. I crawled under the blankets in front of the fireplace and went to sleep.

In the morning, one of them coughed like a tired dog that had been on an all-night possum hunt. "I think I'm sick," he whispered".

"You're what?" I asked.

"I think I'm sick. Feel my head. Do I feel hot to you?"

He sneezed, wiped his nose on the back of his hand and asked, "You got any aspirin?"

He wanted hot tea and cinnamon toast like his mama used to make. I made him get into the one real bed and was on the sofa reading when he appeared in his tee shirt and boxer shorts complaining that it was *too cold* in the bedroom. He lay down beside me and pulled the quilt over him.

Late that afternoon the other one croaked like a constipated bullfrog. "My throat hurts. I have a headache. I can't breed true my node. Can you get me some aspirin, Liana?"

Oh, shit. I brought him a glass of melted snow and one aspirin.

I moved to a chair, letting one have the sofa. Then I pulled a quilt over the one that lay in front of the fire.

"Tracey, do you remember how Mama used to make us chicken soup when we were sick?"

"Yeah, and toasted cheese sandwiches, and she rubbed our chests with Vicks and gave us whisky with lemon juice and honey when we coughed."

"Yeah, she would sing us to sleep. Liana, can I have some Kleenex?"

"Liana, will you make us some hot tea with lots of honey?"

"Liana, can I use your bucket? It's too cold to go outside and pee."

The cabin already smelled like a damned Frat House bathroom on New Year's Eve.

It was Liana this and Liana that until I came unhinged and seriously considered falling on the floor and having a tantrum, but then a wave of nausea hit me. I made a mad dash for the cold bathroom and my blue plastic bucket.

What followed was the week from hell. Our food supply was nearly gone. So were the charcoal for the grill and the wood for the fire. The snow finally stopped, but the wind did not. It whipped over the mountain, piercing and chilling worse than before.

Thankfully the weather gradually warmed up enough for the snow to start melting. The power came back on, we could flush the commode again, and soon the plumber got up the mountain to fix the pipes in the big house.

When the repair man finally made it, he said the kitchen floor would need to be replaced before the twins could move back in. They decided to remodel and called in a designer.

My classes resumed. I learned to make glazes and fire pieces in the kiln. I started making a set of dishes, with matching mugs with our three names on them.

In short, we fell into a comfortable routine. Tristan cooked, Tracy did the dishes, I did the grocery shopping and laundry and we all shared the cleaning. Oggy sat on the sofa, licked his genitals, passed gas and grinned at us like he was watching a Russian Ballet choreographed by George Balanchine.

One day I was doing laundry when all of a sudden it occurred to me that I had missed a period. No, I had missed two periods and—oh hell—I'd lost count. I made an appointment with Dr. Glover.

The old man, with white hair and a beard to match, cocked one bushy eyebrow at me and said, "Congratulations, my dear, you are going to be a mother."

"Oh, shit!"

"Who is the lucky father?"

"The Reynolds twins."

"Oh, I'm sorry, my dear, I have trouble hearing, which one did you say?"

"I don't know. They both moved in with me during the blizzard."

"I'm sorry, my dear. Did you say they *both* moved in with you?"

"They did."

"You slept with *both* of them?"

"Yes sir, I guess I did. I couldn't tell them apart. I can now."

"I understand. I delivered those boys. Their own mother couldn't tell them apart. They went to college together, roomed together and I doubt they have ever spent a night apart in their whole lives. Didn't you use birth control?"

"No sir, I didn't think I needed to. I tried to get pregnant for five years and couldn't. My husband was upset because I was unable to conceive."

"Well, somebody just proved *him* wrong," the doctor chuckled. "Which twin will you marry? Which one do you love?"

"Oh, I love them both. I couldn't possibly choose."

"But what will you do, my dear?"

"I guess I'll have a baby."

I didn't know whether to laugh or cry as I sat on the examination table waiting for the nurse, Mrs. Jordan, to come in with Dr. Glover's instructions. Mrs. Jordan tried to keep a straight face, but couldn't.

"Well, honey, like my grandma used to say, "If it has tires or testicles, it'll cause you trouble." She handed me a sheet of instructions and I could hear her laughing all the way down the hall.

The twins were delighted with the news and they babied me like a hot house orchid. My ex didn't pay this much attention to me in the whole five years we were married, the sorry SOB.

I was nearing my eighth month when the twins took me to see what they had done to the house. The kitchen was a dream: ceramic tile floor, new cabinets, marble countertops and stainless steel appliances.

"We have something else to show you," they said. I was led down a hall with shiny new hardwood floors into adjoining bedrooms. Each room contained matching bedroom suites. One included a baby bed, chest of drawers and changing table.

Next they led me down to the basement. As I neared the bottom, I saw the far wall was hung with three rows of shelves. In front of them sat a potter's wheel and a kiln.

I was two weeks past my due date and in my studio working on the potter's wheel when my water broke. Tracy and Tristan were in their office when I yelled to them to take me to the hospital. We got there about three hours before I delivered a baby boy.

The twins had the whole obstetrical floor in hysterics when they argued about which one he looked like.

The three of us had agreed that if the baby was a boy, they would name it. If it was a girl, I would pick the name.

They had the name already – Thomas David for their father, shortened to T.D.

For the next few weeks we took turns burping, wiping sour spit up, changing smelly diapers and walking the floor in the middle of the night with a colicky baby.

T. D. Reynolds had two stay–at–home dads who designed websites in the office they shared upstairs, while his mama threw pots downstairs.

Tracy and Tristan put a baby seat in the car they shared and everywhere they went, T.D. went too. The child actually believed that having two fathers was normal.

So I had plenty of time to work and establish Reynolds Ridge Pottery. I sold my pots in galleries throughout the mountains. Soon the twins had a lovely sign made and installed down on the main road at the foot of our driveway: *Reynold's Ridge Pottery Ahead.* After that, the buyers came to me.

Needless to say, people were plenty curious about our lifestyle. There was a lot of gossip about what went on up at the Reynolds house, and I hate to imagine what was said when everyone heard I was pregnant again.

At that point, I actually threatened to cut off the twins' dangly things. But then I remembered how little there was to do up here during the lonely winter months and thought better of it.

This time Dr. Glover didn't even raise an eyebrow when I walked into his examining room. But when he placed his stethoscope on my stomach, his eyes grew enormous. "Oh my, I hear two heartbeats, my dear!"

I was in shock when I returned to the waiting room, where Tracy and Tristan were watching T. D. toss toys out of a basket.

Tristan caught my eye, gave me a sidelong smile and blushed. "What did the doctor say?"

I held up two fingers.

He turned to Tracy, an inquisitive look on his face.

Tracy gasped like a beached fish before he was able to say, "I think we're having twins."

I made a snipping motion with my fingers and aimed at their crotches. When looks of sudden shock crossed their faces, I leaned over and whispered, "The doctor says you'll hardly feel a thing!"

MIDLIFE CRISIS

The van with *CAL PUCKET'S PLUMBING SERVICE* written in gold letters pulled in front of *I-Hops* at 7AM sharp, as it did every morning. And Cal, wearing a baseball cap with a confederate flag on it, a plaid flannel shirt and mud-splattered work boots, walked into the restaurant, sat in his usual booth, and waited for Mabel to bring him eight pancakes, a pitcher of maple syrup and coffee in a Pyrex pot from the four-burner Bunn coffee maker.

But today instead, a blonde with hair that smelled like strawberries said, "Good morning, hon."

"Where's Mable?" Cal asked.

"Oh, bless her heart, she had a hip replacement yesterday. What can I git ya, sugah?

Wanda Faye Larson's well-padded behind was stuffed into white pants so tight Cal could see the impression of her panties. He watched her rear end jiggle all the way to the swinging doors with the little round windows at the top, and then it disappeared into the kitchen.

Cal's heart leapt for joy. In a few hours, he would be as free as a bird, and the day couldn't have gotten off to a better start if he had planned it.

He finished his pancakes, had a second cup of coffee, paid the cashier, stuck a toothpick in his mouth, and headed to the attorney's office to sign divorce papers. He'd have to give Florine the house, but hell, it was worth it.

Cal had several repair jobs scheduled, a trip to the plumbing supply store, and after that, he was going Dink's Tavern to celebrate his freedom and get shit-faced drunk.

He finished up a little early and was parking in front of Dink's when his cell phone rang. "Hello?"

"Cal, this is Florine. Now, don't get mad when I tell you this, but I accidently flushed a Tampon down the toilet and it's stopped up."

"My God, Florine, what made you do a fool thing like that?"

"I'm sorry," she cried. "I was rushin' to get dressed and go sign the divorce papers. I was just gettin' up off the commode and….."

"Stop, I don't need no details. Florine, in case you forgot, we got divorced this morning. You can't keep callin' me to run over there to do stuff for you. You just gotta git yourself another plumber."

"Please Cal, help me," she pleaded. "You're the only plumber in thirty miles."

"Okay, I'll be there in a few minutes. In the meantime, if you have to go, use a bucket."

It was going on 8:00PM when he got Florine's toilet unstopped and handed her the bill.

"Cal, you ain't gonna charge *me,* are you?"

"Florine, you can read: Cal Puckett's Plumbing Service, for services rendered: $40.00 for house call and $25.00 per hour."

She was crying when he left, but he headed to Dink's anyway. He was ready to move on with his new life.

After a few beers with the guys at the bar, he drove off feeling wide open and ready to rip, and when he saw the flashing blue light and heard the siren, he realized he'd been rippin' a little too fast.

All he could remember when he woke up in jail, was some asshole telling him to get out of the car, put his hands on the hood, and blow into the breathalyzer. Cal was charged with DUI and given a court date.

The next morning when Wanda Faye came to take his order at I-Hop, she said, "Lord, hon, are you coming down with something? What's wrong, sugah?"

He told her what had happened, and she said, "Do tell, sweetie, I know just what you need."

She handed him a card: *WANDA FAYE LARSON— MASSAGE, MEDITATION AND REFLEXOLOGY.* "I just happen to have an opening tonight, sugah, how does 7:00PM sound?"

Wanda Faye's bedroom was filled with sweet oils, scented candles and she smelled like she had sprayed on gardenia perfume with a garden hose.

"We'll start with your back, sugah. Let's take off your shirt and massage those tight shoulder muscles."

Wanda Faye poured oil on her hands and slowly ran them down his neck and shoulders. Then she said in sweet voice barely above a whisper, "Take some deep breaths, sugah. Breathe in real slow, now breathe out. That's good. Now, you just think of something pleasant. Imagine you are in a boat floating on a calm lake with the most beautiful woman you ever seen. Your body is soothed by the rhythm of the boat rocking back and forth over the water, and her hands are awakening you to feelings you haven't felt in years."

Oh yeah, he thought, as Wanda Faye eased her hands down his back, over his bottom, and down to his feet.

"Now visualize the beautiful woman massaging your toes, releasing endorphins that relieve tension. She stimulates pressure points that increase blood circulation to your private parts. Okay. Now roll over, darlin', and let's make the front feel good, too."

Cal rolled on his back. *Oh Yeah,* he thought as he watched the candle light flicker over Wanda Faye's naked body, all the way down to her bleached-blond pubic hair.

Wanda Faye was staring at the heart tattoo on his chest, with doves holding a waving banner that said: *I love Florine.* All of a sudden, he went numb. He couldn't feel a thing from the waist down. Just when he was ready to make love to the beautiful Wanda Faye Larson, his damned pecker petered out.

His doctor told him this happened to lots of men his age. Damn, he thought, just when I'm ready to *live it up*, I can't *get it up*. The very next day, he got a prescription for Viagra filled and put it in the glove compartment of his truck.

Cal's ex-wife, Florine, who worked as a cashier at Target, spent all day ringing up Christmas presents and stocking stuffers and listening to Christmas music on the intercom. She was depressed and tired of going home to an empty house, so she picked up a six-pack of Budweiser, a bucket of Kentucky Fried Chicken, and headed over to Cal's trailer.

He started to tell her to go away, but when he smelled the fried chicken, he let her in. He drank three beers and turned on the TV to watch a rerun of *Talladega Nights*. On the show, Cal and Ricky Bobby (Shake and Bake) had just finished a race, when Ricky Bobby's assistant, Susan, talked him into going with her to a bar. She was trying to seduce Ricky Bobby, when Florine slid over and put her arms around Cal and started rubbing the inside of his leg. All of a sudden, blood rushed to his groin till he felt like he was gonna burst.

"Cal, honey, maybe the divorce was a mistake," she whispered as she rolled over on top of him.

It was beginning to snow when Cal arrived at I-Hop. It felt good to get in out of the cold. He slid across the green plastic seat and waited for Wanda Faye to bring his coffee. "Morning, sugah," she said as she filled his cup. "How you feelin' this mornin'?"

"I'm feelin' like a new man, Wanda Faye. Bring me two eggs over easy, grits, and toast with some butter and lots of them little packs of grape jelly. And Wanda Faye, I'm feelin' like I need one of your massages, how about it, babe?"

He parked in Wanda Faye's driveway and popped one of the blue pills in his mouth, this time determined to prove his manhood. He grabbed the bag he brought from the ABC store and rang her door bell.

They'd had a couple of drinks when he felt the Viagra working. Wanda Faye lit the scented candles, rubbed oil on her hands and started on his back. Lying on his stomach was becoming too uncomfortable, so he said, "Babe, let's go ahead and do the front."

It was pointing straight up when he rolled over. *Oh yeah,* he thought, but just then his cell phone rang.

"Cal!" Florine screamed. "I got burned bad. Please come help me. I can't afford to call no ambulance. Please come get me, Cal!"

On the way to the hospital, between fits of screaming, Florine told him she had wiped up some spilled gasoline in the carport with a paper towel and had thrown it in the toilet. She lit a cigarette, and was sitting on the toilet smoking and reading the Reader's Digest, when she threw the cigarette butt between her legs. "My butt's burned. I'm ruined, Cal, I'm ruined!"

"I swear to god, Florine, you're crackin' up. When your ass heals, you need to go in for a brain scan. You should know better than to do a fool thing like that."

When they released her from the emergency room, the doctor told Florine to sleep on her stomach for a while and to buy a donut cushion to sit on.

A few days later, Cal was up under a house thawing a frozen pipe when his phone rang. "Now Cal," Florine said in her whinny voice, "don't have a hissy fit, but I need you to put a new seat on the toilet. This one is burned pretty bad."

"Florine, I'll put it on the schedule. I'll be there tomorrow sometime between 3PM and 4PM."

He was taking Wanda Faye to Lineberger's Fish Camp at 5:30, and he made it to Florine's by 4:00. His ex-wife was sitting on her donut in front of the TV, watching Jeopardy.

"Cal, I don't know if I'm ever gonna be a normal again, you know, about sex and all that? My pubic hair is plumb singed off my body. I mean, I'm scared about what I done to myself. I'm in a terrible fix."

"No offense, Florine, but we're divorced, remember? I don't need to know nothin' about your sex life," he said as he handed her a bill: Cal Pucket's Plumbing Service: House call $40.00, toilet seat $30, labor $ 25.

"Cal," she cried, "you gonna charge me again?"

"I got a bidness to run, Florine."

Somehow Cal made it to his date with Wanda Faye on time. They pulled in between a Camero and a pickup truck on the gravel parking lot at Lineberger's. When they entered the restaurant, a fishnet with corks strung through it hung on a brown- paneled wall over a sign that said "Seat Yourself."

A waitress wearing sneakers and an apron with a pocket full of straws dropped a couple of plastic-covered menus on the table, then came back with two Styrofoam cups of sweet tea with lemon wedges half- hidden in the crushed ice.

They both ordered fried flounder, fried shrimp, French fries, hush puppies and slaw—which their waitress carried on a tray held high above her head as she danced her way between tables like a ballerina.

Cal was paying at the cash register, when a man came from the kitchen wearing a grease- splattered apron that hung from a loop around his neck. "Hey Cal, how you doing man? I ain't seen you in a coon's age."

"Jimmy, how's it goin', man?"

"Purty good, how's Florine?"

"She's good. We got divorced, you know. She's kinda lonely. You should give her a call, seeing as to how ya'll went to school together. She'd love to see you."

"I'll do that."

"Where you livin' now, Jimmy?"

"I'm stayin' with Mama and 'em."

A couple of weeks later, when Cal couldn't wait to get home, pop the top on a Bud, and settle down in front of the TV, he saw Florine's car parked in his driveway.

"Cal, honey, you know what day this is?" she asked him.

"It's Tuesday, Florine."

"It's our anniversary, sweetheart. I brought you some beer and a large pepperoni pizza. You got a microwave in there? Come on inside, and let me heat it up a little bit."

"We're divorced, Florine. You don't celebrate when you're divorced."

"I know, honey, but you don't forget anniversaries, neither."

They were watching a rerun of Perry Mason, when Florine said, "I don't know why on earth you told Jimmy Snipes I was lonely. He come over the other night. I never did like him even in high school. What in the world made you think I wanted to get with him? He smells like he's has been standing over a deep fat fryer all day, which he has. If he lives to be a hundred, he'll never get that rancid grease smell outta his hair."

Florine put her head on Cal's shoulder. "Cal, you remember twenty years ago? We were at Myrtle Beach, and I was wearing that fancy little black nightgown I bought for our honeymoon. I think I still have that thing somewheres. I'm gonna see can I find it. You remember what a wonderful night we had in that hot little bedroom right there on the ocean front? Well, it wasn't our first rodeo, but it was real special, wasn't it, sweetheart?"

Florine kissed Cal's cheek and ran her hand down past his stomach, and then on a little further. "Remember what fun we used to have, baby?"

Later, she said, "Cal, honey, didn't that bring back good ole memories? I told you we never shoulda got a divorce. You know how I told you I was worried I might not ever be able to have sex again after I burned my bottom? Well, sweetheart, it was just as good as it was on our honeymoon, and *you* sure ain't got no problems in that area, do you, honey...?

"Cal, say something. Cal, did you even hear one word I said?"

About the Author

Betsey Barber Hampton lives in Davidson, North Carolina. In her early years she was happiest in front of an easel, paint brush in hand. She was interested in anything ART and loved showing her works at various galleries.

Now in her eighties and handicapped, Betsey enjoys writing short stories, doing genealogy and exploring family secrets.

The stories in FAMILY SECRETS are stories about the complexities in the lives of everyday people. They are stories about the fragility of life and the intricate web of experiences woven into them. They are tales of buried secrets when unearthed reveal portraits of betrayal, seduction, and sensuousness, passionate romance.